"If only I could make you understand," Wes said.

"If only I could make you see how much this new life I've found means to me."

Joy touched his cheek lightly with her fingertips. "I know."

"Do you?" he asked softly.

She nodded. "I went looking for love once, and I found it here."

He stood on the porch a long while without speaking. At last he squinted into the darkness. "You've given me a lot to think about."

He went slowly down the steps, then strode off into the night. Joy turned away, unable to watch him go, and hurried inside. She closed the door, then switched off the overhead light and stood there listening as he drove away. Only then did she let herself feel it. Only then did she let it out. "It can't be," she said. "You know it can't be."

Dear Reader,

When I think of the month of June, I summon up images of warm spring days with the promise of summer, joyous weddings and, of course, the romance that gets the man of your dreams to the point where he can celebrate Father's Day.

And that's what June 1990 is all about here at Silhouette Romance. Our DIAMOND JUBILEE is in full swing, and this month features *Cimarron Knight*, by Pepper Adams—the first book in Pepper's *Cimarron Stories* trilogy. Hero Brody Sawyer gets the shock of his life when he meets up with delightful Noelle Chandler. Then in July, don't miss *Borrowed Baby*, by Marie Ferrarella. Brooding loner Griffin Foster is in for a surprise when he finds that his sister has left him with a little bundle of joy!

The DIAMOND JUBILEE—Silhouette Romance's tenth anniversary celebration—is our way of saying thanks to you, our readers. To symbolize the timelessness of love, as well as the modern gift of the tenth anniversary, we're presenting readers with a DIAMOND JUBILEE Silhouette Romance title each month, penned by one of your favorite Silhouette Romance authors. In the coming months, many of your favorite writers, including Lucy Gordon, Dixie Browning, Phyllis Halldorson and Annette Broadrick, are writing DIAMOND JUBILEE titles especially for you.

And that's not all! There are six books a month from Silhouette Romance—stories by wonderful authors who time and time again bring home the magic of love. During our jubilee year, each book is special and written with romance in mind. June brings you *Fearless Father*, by Terry Essig, as well as *A Season for Homecoming*, the first book in Laurie Paige's duo, *Homeward Bound*. And much-loved Diana Palmer has some special treats in store in the months ahead.

I hope you'll enjoy this book and all the stories to come. Come home to romance—Silhouette Romance—for always!

Sincerely,

Tara Hughes Gavin
Senior Editor

ARLENE JAMES

Family Man

Published by Silhouette Books New York
America's Publisher of Contemporary Romance

To Joyce,
with thanks,
not only for the help, but the friendship
and love
D.A.R.

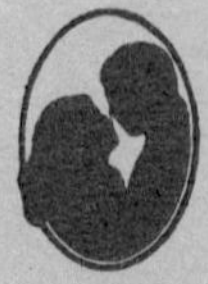

SILHOUETTE BOOKS
300 E. 42nd St., New York, N.Y. 10017

Copyright © 1990 by Arlene James

All rights reserved. Except for use in any review, the reproduction or utilization of this work in whole or in part in any form by any electronic, mechanical or other means, now known or hereafter invented, including xerography, photocopying and recording, or in any information storage or retrieval system, is forbidden without the permission of Silhouette Books, 300 E. 42nd St., New York, N.Y. 10017

ISBN: 0-373-08728-4

First Silhouette Books printing June 1990

All the characters in this book are fictitious. Any resemblance to actual persons, living or dead, is purely coincidental.

®: Trademark used under license and registered in the United States Patent and Trademark Office and in other countries.

Printed in the U.S.A.

Books by Arlene James

Silhouette Romance

City Girl #141
No Easy Conquest #235
Two of a Kind #253
A Meeting of Hearts #327
An Obvious Virtue #384
Now or Never #404
Reason Enough #421
The Right Moves #446
Strange Bedfellows #471
The Private Garden #495
The Boy Next Door #518
Under a Desert Sky #559
A Delicate Balance #578
The Discerning Heart #614
Dream of a Lifetime #661
Finally Home #687
A Perfect Gentleman #705
Family Man #728

ARLENE JAMES

grew up in Oklahoma and has lived all over the South. In 1976 she married "the most romantic man in the world." The author enjoys traveling with her husband, but writing has always been her chief pastime.

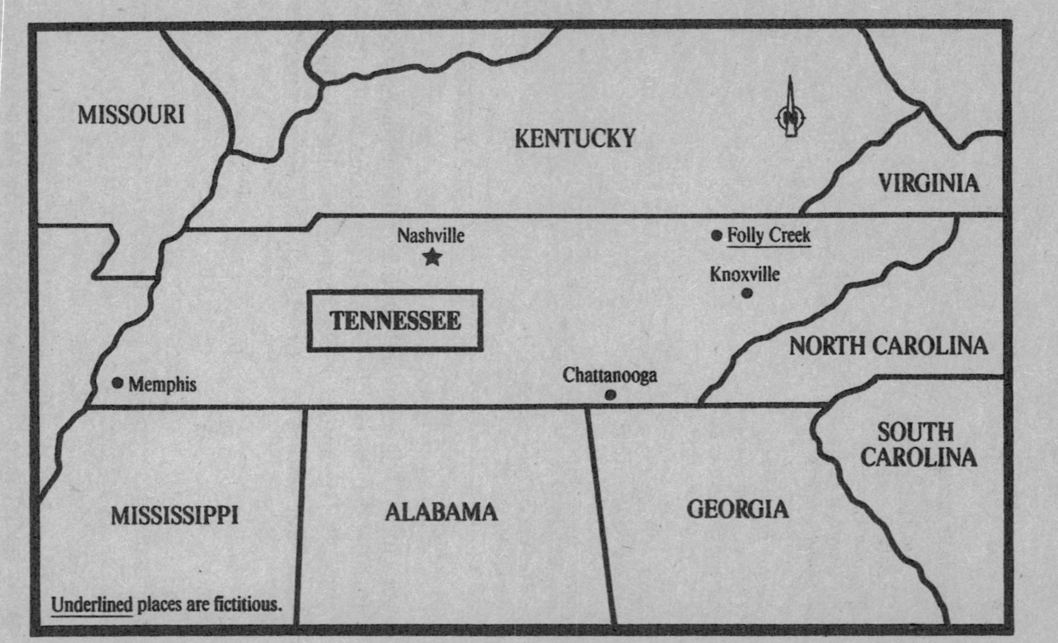
MISSOURI
KENTUCKY
VIRGINIA
Nashville
Folly Creek
Knoxville
TENNESSEE
NORTH CAROLINA
Memphis
Chattanooga
SOUTH CAROLINA
MISSISSIPPI
ALABAMA
GEORGIA
Underlined places are fictitious.

Chapter One

Please, Joy?'' the boy wheedled. ''I'll eat my whole supper, I promise, every bite.''

The young woman behind the counter made a final swipe at the aluminum work surface and dropped the sponge into a small bucket of cleaning solution. It was her own concoction, consisting of equal parts of detergent, disinfectant, and vinegar cut by water, and it was just one of many reasons why her employer, Mr. Ball of Ball's Sundries and Soda Fountain, found her very nearly indispensable. She rinsed her hands and wiped them dry on her apron before reaching across the counter to hug the boy perched on the stool.

''Why don't you have an apple, instead?'' she prodded. The boy's groan was accompanied by the dry rustle of a newspaper from the first of four booths at the end of the fountain bar. Unthinkingly, Joy glanced in the stranger's direction. He was an odd one—good looking, a classy dresser, probably just passing through because she certainly hadn't seen him around before. He was obviously in no hurry. He'd been sitting in that booth for over an hour, sipping coffee and reading the *Folly Creek Crier*, though what he could find in that thin publication to hold his interest, she couldn't imagine. It was a weekly newspaper comprising all of ten pages, which she usually disposed of within ten minutes. But then, to each his own, she always said. Besides, he was pleasant enough, not really friendly but not demanding, either.

"Aw, come on, Joy," the boy was saying, "everything doesn't have to be nutritional, does it? Besides, ice cream's a good source of calcium. That's what my health book says."

She smiled at him and ruffled his hair with her fingertips. "Did it happen to say anything about cholesterol?"

He groaned again and dropped his head onto his folded arms in an exaggerated expression of frustration. Joy laughed and abruptly changed her mind.

"So what kind of ice-cream float did you have in mind?" she asked, and his head popped up.

"All right!"

"Hold on now," she warned. "Don't you be forgetting that you promised to eat your supper, and that means your whole supper, veggies, too."

"Veggies, too!" the boy vowed. "Make it root beer and chocolate!"

Joy put her hands on her hips, considering the combination. "Yuck," she decided, "and this from a kid who gags at the idea of a cooked carrot." She turned away and went quickly to work. When she'd added the root beer for the third time, raking off the head of foam with a spatula, she picked up a can of cream topping and began to shake it. "You won't mind if I fix this up with some whipped cream and a cherry, will you?" she asked innocently.

"Oh, yum!" Her young patron was enthusiastic, as she had known he would be. "Two cherries," he pleaded, "make it two cherries, *please*."

Joy laughed. "Will you listen to that?" she said, dipping into the maraschino jar with a special fork. "Two cherries, no less. You know what your momma would say, don't you? She'd say I've spoiled you stinking, that's what she—" Joy broke off, suddenly realizing what she'd done. Silently, she dropped the second cherry onto the floating island of whipped cream and slid it across the counter to the now glum boy. "Oh, hey," she told him quietly, wanting to bite her tongue, "I am sorry, but you know, honey, there has to come a time when we can talk about her. We can't just go on pretending that she wasn't the smack center of our lives for a time. It hurts to talk about her, it does, but it helps, too."

The boy shoved a straw into the foamy treat and lifted his shoulders, managing a weak smile. "I know," he said. "It's just that sometimes when a thing pains you, you have to do it a little bit at a time."

"That's right," she assured him softly, "one step at a time, and believe it or not, sweetie, a day will come when we won't pine after her so much, and then remembering will be pure pleasure."

"I'll be glad for it," he said, and she ruffled his mouse-brown hair again. He ducked his head and made a determined pull on the straw. Joy turned away and resumed cleaning the work space. She'd made one or two swipes when Mr. Ball came hurrying by, smoothing his thin hair to his head with his palms and calling out for her to watch the place until he returned. She smiled and lifted a dish towel in reply, not that he needed assurance. Joy Morrow was nothing if not dependable; the boy sitting there at the counter proved that. When Joel's mother had taken her in, a runaway at seventeen, she had recognized a good girl driven to the limits of her endurance by a life full of vagaries and difficulty. What Joy Morrow had needed then was the very thing Joel Caudell needed now, stability, and she was determined to provide it for him as his mother had provided it for her over a happy period of six years. With that goal in mind, in the weeks since Cynthia Caudell's death, Joy had determinedly gone about establishing routines and schedules by which she and Joel could live.

So far, so good. Everyone here in town had been supportive of her intentions. Cynthia Caudell had been well known and well thought of, and once her written desires had become public knowledge, people had been quick to extend their hands. Mr. Kincaid, Cynthia's lawyer, had seen to that, but Joy supposed she really had Cynthia herself to thank. Had Cynthia not had the foresight to put down on paper her desire to have Joy remain in the household as Joel's guardian in the event of her death, it was unlikely Mr. Kincaid would have come so quickly to her side. It was a blessing that he had. His support had allowed her to quickly put Joel's fears about his future to rest.

Joel, at first, had been literally consumed by his mother's unexpected death. What twelve-year-old would not have been? Yet, it was doubly difficult for Joel, having lost his other parent while still a toddler. He had been frightened and unsure once he had realized his mother was gone. He had, quite naturally, felt alone. That was a feeling with which Joy Morrow could relate, having lost both of her own parents in an auto accident while she was still in grade school. She remembered so well, even now, the feeling that everyone who had loved her and needed her had just disappeared from the face of the earth as if they had never been.

Immediately after her parents' deaths, she had gone to live with her grandmother, never to return to the little town where every face, every building, every name had been familiar. Robbed of familiarity and pleasure, for suddenly going to Grandmother's had no longer been a treat but a sad and hopelessly final act, she had felt the loss of the safety and security in which childhood flourishes.

In all fairness, she hadn't been the easiest child with which to deal, but from the beginning things had gone awry. Somehow she had become the target of her grandmother's grief. Perhaps it had been her own unwillingness to be satisfied or happy, but more likely it was the fact that she alone had survived the crash that had taken the lives of her parents. For a long while she had felt guilty about that, and yet it hadn't seemed fair that her grandmother had blamed her. True, her only son had died, but her only grandchild had survived, and even without being able to put words to the feeling, Joy had expected her to be grateful for that much. Her own conflicting emotions, combined with her sense of her grandmother's blame, had done nothing to enhance her behavior, and one conflict after another had further separated them, until Joy had finally struck out on her own.

Fearing the hazards of the big city streets, she had set her sights not on Memphis or Nashville or even Knoxville but on the small, gentle towns of beautiful, mountainous northern Tennessee. She had drifted through places with picturesque names like Sunbright and Royal Blue and Smoky Junction and Hickory Star Landing, working at any menial job, earning enough for a meal and a room and another bus ticket, then moving on, looking for some place to belong. She'd found that place in Folly Creek with Cynthia Caudell and her then nearly seven-year-old son.

Cynthia had seen her hanging around town, had watched from a distance while she'd trudged from place to place looking for any kind of work. At the end of a day that had brought her six dollars and fifty cents, Joy had been surprised to find herself involved in conversation with a gentle, pretty woman with brown hair and freckles. She'd been further surprised and grateful to have found herself invited home with that woman.

After dinner and a good night's sleep in a clean, safe room, she'd tried to repay her hostess by cleaning up around the place and making a hearty breakfast for the boy. He was a sweet kid, a little solemn, with his mother's brown hair, fair skin, and freckles and her open, friendly ways. Cynthia had been pleased, but she hadn't made a big deal about it. Instead, she had asked Joy if she'd mind doing a bit of ironing and getting a snack ready for Joel when he came home from school, and then she'd simply gone off to work as she had been doing for years, walking little Joel to school along the way.

Nobody had ever said anything about Joy leaving, so she'd stayed, gradually taking on the housework and the preparation of meals and responsibility for Joel after school. Then, at the end of the semester, Cynthia had laid down the law: Joy was going back to high school, period. She'd made some noises of protest, but secretly she had been thrilled. By the time she'd graduated a year and a half later, they'd been a real family. Joy had gone to work for Ball's Sundries and Soda Fountain and attended college part time, catching a bus over the Cumberland mountain two days a week. She'd made friends, so many friends. Folly Creek was home—sweet, safe home.

Then one dark, cold day, Cynthia had climbed up on a ladder to change a light bulb nested high in the ceiling of the insurance agency office where she worked. The agent and landlord, usually a handy sort himself, had been home nursing an angry bout of flu, so there had been no one on whom she could have called to assist her, and she couldn't open the office until the room was lighted. She had climbed up on that ladder, scared witless by the height and impatient with the phobia, and she had fallen and struck her head. Once again Joy's world had shattered, but this time she had Joel to consider.

Conscientiously, gently, ever mindful of her treasured responsibility, she questioned the boy about his day while he slurped the treat. Had Mrs. Gareth clarified his social studies project? How had math class gone? Had they figured out that tough problem correctly? Once she got him talking, he kept going for a while. Soon, she'd had a blow-by-blow account of the whole day.

Chuck and Sean had gotten into a fight because Molly had told Sean that Chuck had broken her shoe when all he'd really done was accidentally step on the back of it while they were hurrying down the hall. Then Molly and Daphne had had a fight because Daphne liked Chuck and she hadn't appreciated Molly getting him into trouble. Then Chuck had asked *him* to go over and tell Daphne that he didn't appreciate girls who fight, and—would you believe it?—Daphne had slugged him for delivering the message! But then he'd found out that Kathy Epip liked him because she'd railed out old Daphne but good, and could he have enough money for two movie tickets for Saturday night? The gang was going, and he had invited Kathy to join them.

Joy managed not to smile as she pointed out that he'd already seen the movie playing at the one movie house in town, then quickly gave her consent. Kathy Epip was a sweet little girl who'd been working hard to get Joel's attention since fourth grade, when she'd been a tubby little lump of blonde hair and chipmunk cheeks. She wasn't tubby anymore, and those cheeks had turned out to be hiding high, classic bones that gave her a rather sophisticated look. She seemed a perfect sweetheart for a boy rather small for his age, a wounded loner living right on the edge of his thirteenth year. Somehow, he looked a little taller today, a little happier. It made Joy feel warm and snug inside, so much so that she caved in like a cookie castle when he begged to be allowed to meet a friend rather than be made to go straight home.

"He's got a tree house," he argued persuasively, "and I'm the first one he's invited over to see it! Please, Joy?"

"One hour," she told him sternly, "and I'll be calling the house to check and see that you're there."

"You're great, Joy!" he told her, still pulling on his straw. Joy laughed and snapped a towel at him playfully.

"Uh-huh, let's see what you say next time when I turn you down flat."

"I'll say, 'Ple-e-e-ease!' " he intoned comically, and they both laughed.

"Well, it won't do you the least good," she told him. "I'm on to your tricky ways now."

He giggled and sucked up the last of the frothy brown liquid. Just then, the gentleman in the booth folded his paper and got up, snagging her attention. She hurried to the end of the bar, taking up a position behind the old cash register. It was huge and heavy, with keys as big around as nickels and had faintly oriental designs hammered into the tin on the front. She treasured it and kept it gleaming like new.

"Can I get you anything else?" she asked as the man approached.

He shook his head and removed the silver-rimmed glasses from the bridge of his nose. His hair was the color of pine bark, a lightly grayish brown, and worn fashionably short on the sides and at the back. The short parts looked just a shade darker than the top, which was swept back from his forehead and fell in a haphazard center part that somehow managed to look natural and intentional at the same time.

Perhaps the effect was helped along by the gray pinstripe business suit he wore over a white shirt and a silver tie. Not even the town banker wore such an impressive business suit. The stranger dropped the silver-rimmed glasses into his breast pocket and extracted a folded bill from another.

She counted out his change and handed it over with a smile, which evoked an oddly direct stare. His eyes, she noted, were a soft gray-blue—and blank, purposefully so, she sensed. He pursed his lips slightly and laid his folded newspaper beside the register, and then he astounded her by opening his mouth and saying her name.

"Miss Morrow. Miss Joy Morrow."

It was not a question or an introduction, but a simple statement of fact, a revelation of knowledge possessed, and Joy knew instantly that it was somehow ominous. She pushed the cash drawer closed and stared at him, trying to place the handsome, cleanly shaved face. It struck her suddenly as vaguely familiar, and yet...

He pocketed his change and turned away, a wary deliberateness to his movements.

A kind of bemused panic seized her, so that she found herself gripping the corners of the register and watching in helpless angst as he approached the boy.

"Joel," he said, and the boy pivoted on his stool, his face open and inquisitive. "I've looked forward to meeting you." He offered his hand.

The boy gave it a manly shake. "That's fine, mister, but I don't know your name."

The man pulled a breath through flaring nostrils, his jaw working side to side as if he questioned his own judgment, and then he exhaled and seemed to make up his mind. "The name's Caudell," he said, his voice deep as thunder. "Wes Caudell. I'm your uncle."

For Joy the name was like the blows of a hammer. *Wes-Cau-dell. Whack-whack-whack.* Her first thought, strangely, was of a framed photograph that had stood on Cynthia's bedside table and now hung on the wall in Joel's sunny bedroom. The man in that photograph was very similar to the man standing on the other side of the counter, which was understandable as they were brothers. For a moment it was as if Parker Caudell had risen from the grave to claim his son. The reality was no less shocking. This man was family, *Joel's* family.

The boy was staring at him as if he were, indeed, an apparition. Joy gasped, realizing she hadn't breathed for some seconds. Stay calm, she told herself, but even as she did, her pulse began to race. She couldn't think how to react. Her impulse was to run, to get Joel safely away, and for lack of any other option, she acted on it.

"Joel," she said sternly, "go home—*now*."

For a moment the boy merely stared, his face gone pale as winter behind the brown splotches of freckles. Then suddenly, without a word, he slid from the stool, reclaimed his hand, and bolted, snatching up his book bag as he went. Relief swept through her, relief that he had obeyed unquestioningly. But it was short-lived as she looked back at the man standing there before her, naked anger on his face.

"I am that boy's uncle!" he declared accusingly.

"Is that so? Well, I'm that boy's guardian, and you just don't walk up and make an announcement like that!"

"He *is* my nephew!"

"Maybe," she said, knowing it was true but unwilling to acknowledge it. "But that doesn't give you the right to scare the living daylights out of him!"

"I did no such thing! You did that! You put the fear of God into him, ordering him out of here like that. You didn't even give me a chance to explain myself!"

"And what explanation is there for a sudden appearance at this point in his life? You don't have any idea what he's been through!"

"No thanks to you," he retorted, "but I do know now, and that's why I'm here."

Joy heard the bell, but in her confused mind it was the same tinny rattle that had marked Joel's abrupt departure. She didn't even think about Mr. Ball, and if she had, it probably wouldn't have mattered, because she'd suffered enough in her twenty-three years to recognize a threat when she saw one.

"Well, we don't need you here!" she shouted. "Go back where you came from and leave us alone!"

"Who do you think you are," he bawled at her, "keeping me from my nephew?"

"Here now! Both of you!" But not even her boss's voice made her realize he was there. It was only when Mr. Ball's pudgy form came into view that she realized she and Caudell were not alone. She backed off immediately, gulping air and trembling.

"I—I'm sorry," she stammered. "It was the sh-shock."

"Shock was exactly what *I* felt when I found out my sister-in-law had died!" he exclaimed. "Didn't it dawn on you to contact the family?"

"Now you see here, mister!" Ball intervened again. "I won't have you speaking that way to her. I don't know who you are, but I do know Joy here hasn't ever done a wrong thing as long as I've known her, and I don't stand for anybody giving her a hard time. Now you get on out of here before I call in the town law."

Wes Caudell drew himself up very tall, his shoulders square, his chin held at a lofty, stubborn angle. His steel gray eyes glinted, telegraphing an unmistakable message. He cleared his throat.

"My apologies," he muttered tightly, then he turned without waiting for a reply from either of them and strode through the sundries department and out onto the street. The bell clanked hollowly at the end of its chain.

"Humph!" Mr. Ball said. "Some folks, hollering in a public place. What was he saying 'family' for? Cynthia didn't have any family 'cept that boy. I knew her parents as well as I ever knew anybody. They had no family, either of 'em, 'cept her and each other. She went off to college and married that man, and he brought her back here to live in her daddy's place, and he didn't have family, either. Told me so himself. My missus thought it awful sweet they found each other." He shook his head. "That fellow was crazy as a loon, I figure. Good riddance to him."

Good riddance? Joy leaned against the counter, trying to control the speeding thump of her heart. Was it good riddance? Cynthia had said the Caudells didn't count themselves family to her and Joel. They'd opposed her marriage to their elder son, had disinherited him, and when he'd died, not three years later in an accident with heavy equipment, they'd blamed Cynthia and warned her not to look to them for support. But of the second son, her husband's brother, Cynthia had known nothing except that he had asked Parker to postpone the wedding until their parents could be won over, and later he had joined the marines.

Now, like a bad penny, Weston Caudell had turned up again, proclaiming himself uncle and accusing her of keeping his nephew from him when in fact he had never before shown a moment's concern. Whatever his purpose was, he hadn't accomplished it, of that much she was certain. Good riddance? It didn't seem likely.

Reluctantly she informed her employer that Parker Caudell had, indeed, had family and that among them was a brother named Weston. They were people of money, she explained, and there had been bad blood between them. She felt sure that this sudden appearance had frightened Joel, and she wanted to go home to him as quickly as possible. Ball gave his permission, and she left work, hurrying home to find Joel applying himself to his homework, as if nothing at all out of the ordinary had happened, but when he looked up, his freckled forehead was wrinkled with concern. She poured herself a glass of milk and sat down at the kitchen table with him. Its painted top was pockmarked and rough, and doing one's homework there meant moving the paper around constantly to keep from writing over an indentation, but it was such a homey, comfortable place to be that neither Joel nor Joy would have considered moving elsewhere.

Cynthia had made her kitchen table a gathering place. It was here that they had shared meals and games and long, sometimes intense, discussions. It was here that Cynthia had entertained her neighbors and friends, mostly women and an elderly gentleman or two, over cups of coffee and slices of black bottom pie. Joy had asked her once why she never entertained any of the eligible men about town, and Cynthia had smiled and said that she'd had her man and couldn't imagine ever having any other. Joy now wondered how that could have been, unless Parker Caudell had been much less similar to his brother in personality than he had been in physical appearance. Joel, too, had Weston Caudell on his mind.

"Was that man really my uncle?" he asked after she'd had a moment to relax.

She folded her arms against the table top and sighed. "I don't know. But I suppose he is."

Joel bit his lip. "What did he want?"

It was that very question that troubled her, and she didn't have an answer for it. She tried to look unconcerned. "He didn't actually say, but I'm sure it's nothing to worry your head about. Nevertheless, honey, the Caudells gave your parents a hard time, you know, and I don't think your momma trusted them, so we'd better keep our distance, okay? My guess is he'll go away soon enough, just like before."

The youngster nodded, but the way he avoided her eyes told her he knew this matter could not be so easily dismissed. Joel was no fool, after all. He knew Weston Caudell was family—and Joy was not. That fact alone was enough to throw his young life once more into deep turmoil. He shifted his paper to a smooth place and applied his pencil, but in his silent concentration Joy sensed fear and uncertainty and an almost morbid curiosity. She knew just how he felt. It was one more experience they held in common.

Joy didn't have long to worry about when Weston Caudell would turn up again. He came the very next morning, only minutes after Joel had set out for school. Joy had wanted to hold the boy back, to keep him safely within her sight, but she knew Joel needed continuity in his life now as never before, and she couldn't reconcile keeping him home with the lack of concern she pretended. Besides, she couldn't keep him locked up in the house for long. Maybe, she reasoned, if they carried on with their normal lives, life would carry on as normal—but deep down she knew better, and she wasn't really surprised to find Weston Caudell on their doorstep. It stood to reason that he would find the little white house with the yellow trim that stood high on the hillside. Anyone in town could have told him where to find the place, and someone obviously had.

"We have to talk," he said the instant his face came into view.

"I don't have to do anything," she retorted, and attempted to close the door, but he stepped forward, quick as a flash, and stopped her.

"Yes, you do," he insisted, blocking the door with his forearm. "Come on, Miss Morrow, use your head. He's my nephew, for Pete's sake."

"Just leave us alone!" she said, pushing again, not that it did her any good. The door might as well have been blocked by a brick wall, and if that wasn't enough, he lobbed a particularly effective grenade.

"I could just haul you into court, you know."

She didn't know it, but she suspected it was true, and being suddenly confronted with the possibility made it seem real enough. Folks put a great deal of store on blood family, and she didn't want it said that she hadn't given Weston Caudell an opportunity to make his case. She straightened up and squared her shoulders, stepping back from the door.

"That's better," Caudell said, coming fully into the small living room. He took time to look around while smoothing the lapels of his cream-white sport coat and straightening the brown tie that matched the brown pleated slacks and the soft brown shoes, as well as the double stripe in the tan windowpane checked shirt. He tugged at his cuffs and hooked a forefinger into his collar, his eyes—less gray than blue today, she noticed—blandly finishing their assessment. Once done, however, they gave no clue as to his opinion. "We need to have a calm, rational conversation about Joel and what's best for him," he said. "May I sit down?" Without waiting for a reply, he walked across the room and seated himself in one corner of the sofa.

"Make yourself comfortable," she muttered cryptically, and folded her arms. He crossed his legs, and she couldn't help noticing how out of place he looked and how worn the blue tweed cover of the couch seemed. She lifted her chin defensively, imagining what he must think of the place with its faded, flowered drapes and the squeaky old floorboards beneath the braided rug, the crocheted covers on the rickety, mismatched tables and the sagging mantel of the fireplace, its opening filled by a black iron wood-burning stove.

It was a small house with more kitchen than anything else and a third bedroom in the attic, to which access could be had through a narrow open stair in the closed-in porch off the back. It drooped in places and peeled in others, but it was sound and homey and tight, and from that attic bedroom window one could see over the tops of the trees and down into the little valley where Folly Creek meandered. It was a lovely view: shimmering in summer where the light picked up the gleam of water, all red and gold in autumn with leaves piled in banks along the edges of the narrow road, stark in winter and lushly green in spring, as it was now with trees budding and the underbrush already threatening to overwhelm the beaten paths. For six years of her life she had soaked up that view, lying on her bed under the eaves. She was on home ground. Weston Caudell was the one out of place. That thought in mind, she faced him with renewed determination. He seemed unfazed.

"I would have been here sooner," he said, "if I'd known."

"And just how did you find out?" she shot back, refusing to feel guilty for not having been the one to deliver the news.

He folded his hands together and gave her a stern look meant, no doubt, to quell. "I have my ways," he told her flatly. "Let's just say I found out from a concerned third party and leave it at that."

This was unexpected. Kincaid had warned her that someone might intervene, but she hadn't believed anyone truly cared for the boy other than her. Why would a third party want to take the boy from her? It didn't make sense. She didn't believe it. Nevertheless, she felt a sudden need to sit. She took one quick step to the side and dropped abruptly onto the armless rocker, crossing arms and legs to show she wasn't intimidated.

"I don't believe you," she said, an edge to her voice.

He picked a piece of lint off the sharp crease of his slacks, then fixed her with a frank gaze. "I don't care whether you believe me or not. I care that my nephew is well and happy and has his needs met."

She didn't know if that was good or bad, but she was determined to be hopeful. "So you're here to decide for yourself whether or not I'm good for Joel."

He pursed his lips. "You might say that."

"Well, I'm surprised you'd even bother," she said, "considering that you never did before."

"Just because you didn't know about it doesn't mean I didn't do it," he came back. "Do you think I wouldn't have stepped in if Cynthia had failed to care for the boy?"

"And how would you have known?"

"As I said, I have ways."

"And as I said, I don't believe you."

"You should."

Joy went cold, but she was not to be so easily cowed. She tilted her head to one side, eyeing him blatantly. "How can you expect me to believe you when you offer no proof?"

"My source prefers to remain anonymous," he said. "Let's just say that someone in a position to know has written me regularly with news of my nephew since shortly after his father died."

"And why would that someone do such a thing?" she queried skeptically.

"Because I asked him to."

"Him?"

His face colored slightly, but he ignored the tiny slip and carried on. "I assure you my source is impeccable and quite thorough. I knew, for instance, within a matter of days when you first arrived in Folly Creek."

"You and the whole town," she quipped sarcastically.

"And did the whole town know when you re-established communication with your grandmother?"

Joy felt the flutter of her pulse. Who would know that or care except the small circle of her friends? Yet it wouldn't be too difficult to discover, if a body was willing to ask discreetly. What else had been discreetly ferreted out? When? A thick, sticky lump rose in her throat, and she swallowed it down with some effort.

"All right," she said. "So you know about that. What of it?"

"I'm merely trying to make a point," he said evenly. They both knew he'd made it. Joy licked her lips, needing to score a point of her own.

"Joel needs continuity in his life," she pointed out. "I am that continuity. I make him feel safe."

He waved a hand dismissively. "Given time, I can do the same thing."

"Can you?" she demanded. "I don't think so. All right, so you kept track, and maybe you already know this, but I'm going to tell you anyway. I was a seventeen-year-old runaway. Cynthia took me in, gave me a home, made me part of a family again. She made me feel safe and wanted and appreciated, and that helped me to grow up, and all the time she and Joel were loving me, I was loving them. That's what I've done ever since I've been here, six good years. Now let me ask you something? If you cared so much, why didn't you come forward? And before that, when your parents were cutting your brother up in little pieces, where were you then, Weston Caudell? Tell me that."

His blue eyes went cold gray, and for a long, silent moment Joy feared she had gone too far, struck the mark too deeply. It occurred to her suddenly that she was alone here with this man, that if he chose to harm her, he could. Then, suddenly, he dropped his gaze and ran a hand through his hair, and she wasn't afraid anymore, not of physical harm anyway.

"After I graduated from college," he told her quietly, "I enlisted in the Marine Corp. It was my way of declaring my independence, I suppose. It seemed significant at the time, proof positive that I was my own man. My father saw it as rebellion, and he was probably right. When my brother married, I was stationed in Italy. It was two years before I returned to the States. My parents were absolutely adamant about not discussing Parker or his family, and I let them convince me it was for the best, but my brother's son has never been far from my thoughts, I assure you, and when Parker died, I arranged to have news of him from time to time."

"Well, you may have thought of him, Mr. Caudell," she said icily, "and you may have kept in touch with someone who could give you news of him, but you weren't here—and I was."

"Oh, really?" he came back. "And all this time you've concentrated only on him? Not on school or friends or work or clothes or anything but Joel, right?"

"I didn't say that."

"You're not his mother."

"I never said I was."

"You're not his sister."

"Neither are you!"

"You're not even his aunt!"

She didn't miss the implication, and something told her this was what it would all come down to in the end. Well, she couldn't do anything about blood, but neither could he do anything about feeling, and that's where they stood. Stiffly, she rose and drew herself up to her full five-feet-three inches. She lifted her chin, and her plump, honey-blond pony-tail bounced saucily.

"There are people in this town who will stick up for me," she told him evenly. "I have a good reputation here. People think of Joel and me as family."

"But you aren't," he rebutted coolly.

"I've dropped out of college," she pressed, "and gone to work full-time at Ball's store."

"And you feel that will provide adequate income for the two of you?"

"We're talking about more than adequate income!" she flared. "I know you've got money, but that doesn't mean a thing. *I've* held him while he cried. *I've* sat by his bed at night when he was ill. I've cleaned and cooked for him and seen to it that he got his homework done. I've been at the basketball games, the holidays, the school programs, the church services. I've been here, and I've cared! And you can't take that away by simply saying you're family."

Weston Caudell sighed and stood up, tugging at the tail of his coat. "All right, but there's another side, you know. You're young, very young. You have no children of your own and no experience as a parent, especially as a parent of an adolescent. You have a low-paying job, no savings, no insurance, nothing. This old house isn't even yours. It's Joel's, and without him, you don't even have a place to stay. Now that in itself can be a pretty compelling motive—"

Joy gasped, so taken aback by this new implication that her hand simply came up and struck out by its own volition. The crack it made when it connected with his cheek echoed through the empty house, and the silence that followed was all the more shocking for the sound that had preceded it. Even as the stain rose to the surface of his skin, she steeled herself for the repercussion, feeling certain this time that she had goaded him beyond his endurance. Yet, as she watched, a muscle twitched beneath the imprint of her hand, then stopped, going slack, and he shook himself as if he could shake off anger like a sudden chill. Slowly, he turned his head, facing her once more.

"If you stand between us," he said quietly, "you deprive Joel of knowing his family and you force me to fight for him."

"His mother wanted him to be with me!" she insisted. "She wanted me in her will as Joel's guardian. You can't take him away from me!"

"I can," he stated flatly, "and I will if you force me to. I'm hoping that won't be necessary. I'm hoping you'll stop and think long enough to realize how much I can give that boy, and I'm not talking just about money. I'm talking about real family, about belonging, about identity, about security." He cast another glance about the room, as if to say he found it as lacking as he found her, and then he walked casually to the door, opened it and turned back to her, his hand on the knob. "Think about it," he said, "and while you're at it, think about this: I have all the time in the world, all the time money can buy—and everything else."

He stepped through the door and pulled it closed. Joy listened to his footsteps as he crossed the sloping porch and descended the three steps that led to the uneven stone walkway, and afterward until the sound faded away into silence. Then she sat down again, put her hands to her face and quietly cried.

Chapter Two

Are you saying I don't have a case?'' she asked the lean gentleman folded into the chair across from her. Mr. Kincaid shook his head, one bony knee braced against the rim of his desk.

''There are several factors in your favor,'' he stated carefully, a lawyer to the marrow, ''and there are several factors in his favor.''

''And you won't predict which one of us might come out top dog, will you?''

He laid a long finger alongside a long nose, his lawyer's mind accessing every available scrap of information. His conclusions drawn, he cleared his throat and hunched his shoulders. ''A lot depends on the judge who hears the case,'' he said. ''If we get a judge who lays a lot of store in the intentions of the deceased parent, we shouldn't have a problem.''

''And if we don't?''

He shrugged. ''I'd call it a toss-up.''

Joy braced her elbows against the edge of his desk and rested her chin on her crossed wrists, trying to find a spot of sunlight among the darkening clouds. "Don't Joel's feelings count for anything?" she asked. "I thought kids past a certain age were allowed to say who they wanted to be with."

"They are," he assured her. "They don't have complete say in the matter, of course, but their opinions weigh heavily."

"Well, that's something," she said, dropping her hands and forcing a confident tone. Kincaid gave her his noncommittal smile and templed his bony fingers.

"You know, this thing doesn't have go to go court. There's lots of room for compromise here, and Caudell's attorney will no doubt advise him of that. I wouldn't worry too much."

Her own smile was thin and weak. She had seen Weston Caudell, talked to him, and he didn't seem the compromising type, but there was no point in borrowing trouble. She already had more than enough of that.

She thanked Kincaid and left him, hurrying back to the store without taking time for lunch. She didn't want to take advantage of Mr. Ball's generosity. She had to be careful just now. The term was, she believed, *above reproach*.

Back at the shop she spent the afternoon telling herself that everything was all right. Should the matter ever go to court, Joel would simply tell the judge that he wanted to be with her, and the judge would take a look at her unblemished record, note her accomplishment and Cynthia's recorded wishes, and that would be that. On the other hand, Caudell might back off. He had to know her case was at least as strong as his, and when he realized Joel's preference could not be swayed, it was likely that he would simply lose interest and go on about his business. Meanwhile, she decided, she and Joel were simply going to carry on as if Weston Caudell had never even appeared in Folly Creek.

He did not lose interest, and he did not go away. In fact, over the next couple of weeks Weston Caudell made himself very much a part of the local scene. Everywhere she and Joel went, he was there. He turned up at church, at baseball games, even at the movie house when Joel and his friends were there for their group "date." She heard through the grapevine that he was living out at the Shady Grove Motel and was looking for a house to rent. The whole community was abuzz with talk about this new arrival. He was called a financier, an entrepreneur, but praised for being "down to earth" and "a regular fellow." Suddenly everyone knew about Weston Caudell and his reasons for being in Folly Creek. To a lot of folks it was as if the twentieth century had walked in on two legs.

"Carries around a computer in a briefcase," Joy overheard one man saying at her soda counter. "Plugs it into a telephone, and there's his office right there. Beats all I ever seen."

A second man commented as how Caudell had told yet a third that the stock market was not the place for the average individual to invest. "Too complicated," he said. "The thing is bonds and mutual funds."

She turned away in disgust. It wasn't as if either one of the fools knew a mutual fund from a wood sprite, but if Weston Caudell had said it, it must be so. After all, he had a computer he could plug into a telephone.

It was all Joy could do to be civil to the man whenever she saw him, but he displayed a cheerful good humor that seemed never to fail at these "accidental" meetings, which, of course, made her want to throttle him. Nevertheless, she had little choice but to play his game by his rules. She counseled Joel to simply ignore the man, and the boy tried, goodness knew, but Weston Caudell was not an easy fellow to ignore. He was confident and friendly with the boy, not too pushy, not too aloof, so that failing to respond to his overtures seemed downright rude. With Joy he was polite and quiet, his gaze direct, bold, sometimes challenging, sometimes speculative. She realized early on that he knew what he was up to, and maintaining a cordial distance seemed her only possible course—at least in public. In private, she decided, a planned confrontation might be the wiser course, but she had to pick her moment.

She decided the moment had come on the third Sunday she and Joel attended church in the smilingly irritating company of "that fine Caudell man," as Preacher Pritikin Marsh himself was heard to say. It was simply too much, having Weston Caudell thrust at her everywhere she went, so she calmly arranged for Joel to go home with a friend for Sunday dinner. As soon as the boy was safely away, she cautiously approached Caudell as he conversed with Preacher Marsh. She waited, smiling benignly at their nods of recognition, but Weston did not immediately grant her his attention. Indeed, he seemed to promptly forget that she was even there, effectively condemning her to wait with her hands folded demurely as she shifted from one foot to the other and watched thc parking area empty. At last, her patience exhausted, she interrupted the two men.

"Could I have a word with you, Mr. Caudell?" she asked firmly. Preacher Marsh sent Weston an inquisitive look, received an affirmative nod, cleared his throat and excused himself. Weston smiled easily and cast a glance upward at the noontime sun. The spring weather was holding clear and cool, but the sun was dazzlingly bright. He lifted a hand and indicated the enormous oak that stood at the edge of the dusty road.

"Let's talk in the shade, if you please."

Joy looked around, realizing that they were quite alone except for a few stragglers remaining inside the church. The enormous trunk of the stately oak would screen them from all but the most direct presence. She nodded and turned, leading the way down the narrow gravel path. When they reached the tree, she primly ducked beneath the low-hanging branches and strolled around to the side facing the road. Caudell followed uncomplainingly, his lips pursed in silent speculation. Joy put her back to the tree. Caudell clasped his hands behind him, his blue-gray eyes narrowing. Joy took in a deep breath through her mouth, ordering her words in her mind and preparing to speak, when he jumped the gun on her.

"I'm glad you're ready to talk," he said suddenly, his voice light and soft. "We sort of got off on the wrong foot, and I've felt bad about that."

This was surprising, but not altogether convincing. She folded her arms. "Oh, really?"

He nodded. "In fact, I've been thinking that we really ought to be friends. After all, we both want the same thing."

She was truly amazed, and she let it show. "You think we should be friends?"

He leaned an elbow against the tree trunk and scratched his ear. "Well, I think we should be friendly. We're adults, after all, and it is just possible that we both want whatever is best for Joel."

She inclined her head skeptically. "One of us wants what's best for Joel, the other one just thinks he does."

He dropped his arm and leaned into the tree with his shoulder. "You don't know what I think," he said, "and you probably wouldn't believe me if I told you."

"What do you think?"

He gave her a long, measuring look. "Well, for one thing," he said, "you're really quite lovely." Joy was simply taken aback. She gaped at him, while a slow, sheepish grin spread across his face. "I mean it," he told her. "I like your hair that way. It's rather chic." He chuckled, apparently as surprised with himself as she was.

Joy clamped her mouth shut, appalled to find herself blushing with pleasure. "My, um, hair is not the issue," she told him coolly, pushing at the honey-gold locks with her hand.

His smile became strained, and his gaze flitted to the branches overhead. "I didn't think you'd mind a compliment," he said. "Beautiful women rarely do."

Joy rolled her eyes. "You must think I'm awfully gullible."

"Not at all," he insisted. "It's just that I've had a chance to see you turned out several different ways now, and I must say each one seems more fetching than the last. I can't help wondering," he went on pointedly, "if it's intentional."

This time her chin dropped almost to her chest. *Intentional? Intentional!* He thought she'd been making herself attractive for him? "Tell me something," she snapped. "How do you manage under the weight of such an overinflated ego?"

He laughed as easily as if the words had been innocent banter. "I have broad shoulders," he came back.

"So did Frankenstein."

He put his back to the tree and folded his arms, turning his head to look at her. "I wouldn't mind if it had been intentional," he told her, and she shook her head, truly awed at the man's audacity, his sheer nerve.

"I don't know what you expect to accomplish with this nonsense," she said, "but it isn't working."

He sighed and bowed his head. "One of these days," he told her, "you're going to realize it's better to have me as a friend than an enemy. I can be either one, but I'd rather be a friend. Be reasonable, why don't you? I'm housebroken, and I don't bite. I can eat in public without embarrassing anyone, and you won't find my face on the post office wall."

"Well, gee, I'm sold. What else could a girl ask for?"

"And I'm patient," he added.

Now they were getting to it. Joy turned her shoulder into the tree and fixed him with a hard stare. He accommodated her by raising his head to meet her gaze. "You can be as patient as Job," she said evenly, "but that won't get you Joel."

He gazed at her a moment from beneath drawn, jutting brows. "Now if you were sure of that," he said, turning so that his shoulder rested heavily against the rough bark of the tree, "we wouldn't be having this conversation, would we?"

Joy was taken aback at that. Her color flooded into her cheeks and her bottom lip quivered.

Then a strange thing happened: the smile slid off his face, and he suddenly diverted his gaze.

For one short moment she felt a thrill of triumph, then almost before she knew what had happened his steely-blue eyes pinned her bluer ones. At the same time he shifted his weight, leaning closer, his six-feet-and-more looming over her. She had the sudden impression that he was going to touch her. She almost felt his hands upon her arm, her cheek. Then, oddly, he seemed to think better of the impulse. His gaze shifted to the part in her hair. The hand that hovered near her face moved to slide down the back of his head, coming to rest against his collar. He relaxed, putting space between them, and smiled gamely.

Joy realized for the first time that she was holding her breath, and her lips parted as she carefully drew air. She lifted her chin, dismayed to feel herself trembling.

"Why can't you go away and leave us in peace?" she demanded raggedly. He thumped a forefinger against his breastbone thoughtfully.

"Would you, if you were in my place?"

She stared at him. Both of them knew the answer, but she wasn't going to give him the satisfaction of saying it aloud. "If you truly want what's best for Joel," she said, "you'll leave him alone. He needs to get his life in order again, and he can do that best in familiar surroundings with someone he loves."

"Agreed," he admitted tersely.

She sucked in her cheek, clamping its soft inner side between her teeth, an old habit in moments of stress. Was it possible that he really understood? Could she convince him? "Joel needs me," she told him softly. "I need him."

"I know just how you feel," he replied, and reached up to swat a clump of leaves with one hand. "I've wanted to know my brother's son from the moment he came into this world, but I didn't have the courage to go against my parents while Parker was still living. His death sort of galvanized me, I guess, but then I couldn't very well force myself on Cynthia after the way my family had treated her, so I did the only thing I felt I could—I watched from afar. But now she's gone, too, and I can't just turn my back. He's my nephew. He's my brother's son."

Why did that have to make such sense? She told herself it didn't matter. Joel was the one to be considered here. But despite everything she couldn't help feeling sorry for him. Nevertheless, Wes Caudell was an adult, and as an adult he would have to deal with his disappointments as best he could. Joel was a boy, and he'd had more difficulty in his young life than anyone should have. He deserved her first consideration, not Weston. She pressed her spine against the tree trunk, her head held high.

"Cynthia's out of the way," she told him calmly, "but I'm not, so don't think you can force yourself on that boy now, because I won't have it."

"That's not what I'm trying to do at all," he insisted quietly. "I don't have to force myself on him, and do you know why? Because I'm family. Because I'm his father's brother, and he can't help wanting to know me. That's the natural order of things, and nothing you can do or say will change that."

She stared at him, rocked clear down to the center of her being, for once again she feared he was right. God help her if he was, because if he was, then all he had to do was hang around until Joel's curiosity got the best of him. And so far he had everyone he'd met thinking what a swell fellow he was, no small thanks to Preacher Marsh.

Preacher Marsh. It hit her suddenly. Of course. Who else was privy to every joy and difficulty in their lives? Who else could observe and query with impunity? She began to remember the thousands of interested questions he'd asked, the unannounced visits, and never once had she suspected.

"Marsh is your connection," she said suddenly. "He's the one!"

Weston gave her a bland look. "Pritikin was kind enough to keep an eye on the boy for me," he admitted. "He never interfered, had only the best to say about Cynthia. It was an act of kindness, nothing more."

Joy felt betrayed, and she knew Cynthia would have felt the same way. To have their own pastor playing spy, ready to denounce them at the slightest misstep. "What did he tell you about me?" she demanded.

He slipped his hands into his pockets, obviously trying to maintain his calm composure, and lifted his shoulders in a shrug. "He said you were young, pretty, hardworking, emotional—"

"Emotional!"

He lifted both brows at her outburst, as if to say she'd just confirmed the assessment. She wanted to bite her tongue, but she wasn't about to give him the satisfaction. That slow grin widened his mouth.

"It's not exactly a crime."

"It's not exactly true, either!"

He laughed, his eyes crinkling at the corners. "He also said you ought to be finding a man of your own and making babies."

Joy gasped. "He didn't!"

Weston disciplined a smile, his hand coming up to stroke his chin. "Okay, so Preacher Marsh is a bit of a chauvinist, but then a lot of people can't understand why a pretty girl like you isn't having herself squired around town on one eligible elbow after another. Come to think of it, neither can I."

She glared at him. "I'm not a *girl*!"

He lifted one hand and placed it flat against the tree trunk just above her shoulder, his grin twisting. "So I've noticed."

Her breath caught, her heart doing a slow, heavy thud in her chest. Was he really making a pass at her? He couldn't be making a pass at her. How could he think she'd even consider...

His other hand drifted up and hovered near her shoulder, his fingertips lightly stroking her hair. Suddenly she knew what this was about. A trick. A trap. He was trying to get her to do something she shouldn't. He needed something to use against her, one misstep, one instance of poor judgment. Her bright eyes narrowed. Her chin came up at a sharp angle.

"I'm not some silly girl," she reiterated, "and I don't need some conniving man complicating my life. I have things to do, someone to do them for, and every reason in the world to go on, so why don't you just leave me alone?"

He took his hand away, his grin neither so bright nor so quirky, and inclined his head to one side. "I thought we'd covered that topic pretty well," he said, the lightness of his tone absolutely infuriating.

Joy held herself sternly in check, allowing only the thinnest of smiles to curve her lips. She kept her gaze level and hard, and after a moment he dropped his hand and drew back.

"Go home, Caudell," she told him, standing away from the tree. "Let us be." And then she turned and stalked away, nothing settled, nothing solved, but with her head held high.

The feeling of confidence she took away with her from that Sunday meeting did not remain, however. She could not help feeling uneasy about Preacher Marsh's obvious support of Weston. He seemed a powerful ally in such a small, conservative community, and his long involvement in the matter seemed proof of Weston Caudell's intelligence and skill as an opponent, to say nothing of his commitment to his cause. The sense of betrayal that she felt abated a bit, but she still didn't know what to say to the preacher when he came to visit her one evening unannounced, and what he had to say to her was not particularly comforting.

Basically, he told her that he was neutral as far as the custody issue was concerned. He defended his past involvement by saying that in all the years he had corresponded with Weston there had never been the slightest hint of impropriety or the smallest threat to Joel's happiness. To his mind, he had performed a service of compassion for a man who wanted only to be assured that his nephew was well.

"I never dreamed that the situation could change," he told her. "Who could have foreseen the tragedy? I never expected to have to write and tell the man his sister-in-law had died. I delayed for weeks, hoping you would think to inform the family yourself. I should have realized you'd be too distraught."

"Frankly, it never occurred to me," she said. "Informing the Caudells was the very last thing on my mind."

He nodded, mumbling that he supposed this was natural. "After all, you didn't know Weston was concerned." He went on to explain that he found it not only natural but commendable that Weston had such concern for his nephew, and he had no doubt that Wes would be a fine guardian. He stressed the fact that in his opinion Joy, too, would be quite capable of caring for and guiding the boy, but he wondered if that would be best for Joy herself.

"You're young," he said. "You ought to be enjoying yourself, finding yourself a man, building a home and a family."

"I have a home," she told him stubbornly. "Joel's my family. I don't need or want a man, thank you, and I like my life just fine."

He sighed and shook his head as if dealing with a recalcitrant child. "It's your life," he said. "You have the right to live it any way you choose, but just remember that Weston Caudell has rights, too."

After that, she and the pastor parted on rather stiff but cordial terms. She was shaken to her core by the knowledge that he'd kept Weston informed, but she understood that he'd felt it was a harmless act of compassion he'd performed. Nevertheless, their conversation had done nothing to comfort her growing unease. In fact, as the week wore on, the sense of impending doom deepened and darkened. She couldn't seem to shake the feeling that something dreadful was about to happen, and on Thursday it did.

It was early in the evening, and Joy stood at the kitchen counter, washing lettuce for a salad for their dinner. Joel sat at the table, a science book open before him, a pencil in his hand, pecking at a sheet of lined paper. Sensing his restlessness, Joy sent a glance over her shoulder in his direction.

"You don't seem to be concentrating," she commented lightly, and the boy closed his book, settling into his chair with a sigh. "Something else on your mind?"

For a long moment he said nothing, and this in and of itself told her that she had guessed correctly. She placed the lettuce in a plastic colander and left it sitting in the sink as she dried her hands on her apron.

"Want to talk about it?" she asked, coming to sit with him at the familiar old table. He chewed the inside of his cheek, a habit he'd picked up from her, then his eyes shot up to meet hers.

"He's not so bad, really, Joy—Uncle Wes, I mean."

She knew suddenly that this was exactly what she'd feared—and exactly what Weston Caudell had intended—but she managed to keep her voice steady and her head clear.

"You've spoken with him then?"

He nodded guiltily, his eyes leaving hers for the surface of the table. "I know you said we oughta stay away from him. It's just that I sort of got to feeling sorry for him, and anyway, it isn't as if he's done anything bad. And I was kind of curious, you know, because don't you think he looks a lot like that picture of Dad?"

Joy forced down a rising sense of panic, Caudell's words echoing in her head. *I don't have to force myself on him. He can't help wanting to know me.* Her heart was beating rapidly and with alarming force, but she made herself behave calmly.

"Joel, are you wondering what it would be like to go and live with him?"

"No!" he exclaimed. "No way! I don't want to go anywhere. But..." He bit his lip, obviously pondering the best approach. "The thing is, he can't be too bad. He's spent all this time just getting me to talk to him. I mean, he must really want to know me, and..." He shrugged. "I don't see what it can hurt."

Joy felt as if there were a time bomb ticking away in some forgotten corner of her life, and she wasn't foolish enough to believe that it had gotten there all on its own. She knew all too well who she had to thank for this suddenly very real and present danger, but it was obvious Joel would not agree. What was she to say? How was she to argue? Weston Caudell had already made important progress in pressing his case. Painting him as the blackguard now might well serve simply to alienate Joel at a time when she especially needed to keep him close. She didn't know what else to do except play along and try to keep the upper hand. She sighed and struggled for a serene tone.

"Perhaps your uncle does care for you, Joel," she admitted reluctantly, "but if you really don't want to go and live with him, you shouldn't get his hopes up, should you?"

"I don't want to get his hopes up," the boy said ingenuously. "I just think we ought to be nice to him."

Joy swallowed hard. "Nice to him. A-all right. We can manage that, surely."

The boy fairly collapsed into his chair, his relief painfully evident. "Oh, boy, I was afraid you'd be mad at me."

Despite her fear a genuine smile crossed her face. "No, silly, of course I'm not mad."

"Man, I'm glad about that," he said, "because it just seems so mean to keep on ignoring him."

Joy felt her smile fade. "Well, it's never right to be mean, Joel, but you mustn't feel guilty about...about...well, being uncomfortable with him."

"Oh, I'm not uncomfortable with him," he said offhandedly. "Actually, I kind of like him. Everybody likes him." He glanced upward as if realizing he'd just made an embarrassing blunder, and squirmed in his chair. "Uh, well, not everybody, I guess."

She knew who the exception was. She reached across the table and squeezed his wrist. "It's not that I don't like him," she explained gently. "It's just that I don't know him very well. It's hard to trust someone when you really don't know him, and that's why I think . . . well, I think you should be careful until we know what he's really like, you see?"

"That makes sense." He nodded, apparently giving it some real thought. Joy relaxed a bit, resisting the urge to wipe a hand across her brow. Then suddenly the boy brightened, his eyes going wide, spine straightening. "I know," he said. "I'll invite him over."

Her buoyed hopes came crashing down. "Over?" she repeated dully.

The boy fairly beamed. "You said we ought to get to know him."

"Well, yes. I mean . . ." She tried not to panic, realizing too late how much she'd ceded. She sat there staring at Joel's childish, freckled face, a number of distressing thoughts tumbling through her head. Was he really almost thirteen? He seemed such a child, such an innocent. And how empty her life would be without him! "Do you want to know your uncle better?"

Joel shrugged his shoulders as if surprised she even had to ask. "Sure."

"I see." She took a deep breath. "All right."

"Then he can come over to visit?"

She focused on the tabletop, struggling to get out the words she knew she had to say. "If th-that's what you w-want."

"Oh, Joy, thanks! This is great!" He got up and threw his arms about her neck, missing the look of frightened worry that creased her brow. "I'll ask him tomorrow. Won't it be fun? Man, I never even thought about having an uncle. It's something, isn't it?"

She listened to him babble, but it was Weston Caudell's words she heard. *I'm his father's brother, and he can't help wanting to know me. That's the natural order of things, and nothing you can do or say will change that.* And it was all true. Weston Caudell was slowly stealing everything away from her, the good wishes of the town, the confidence of her own pastor, the affection of this boy who was both friend and family, and, coincidentally, the only real home she had known since her girlhood. And there wasn't a thing in the world she could do about it. She'd have laughed if she hadn't been so perilously close to tears. As it was, she could only lie through the smile on her lips, pretend all was well, and put her trembling hands to tearing the lettuce.

Chapter Three

The day had been a complete waste. Mr. Ball was a bit irritated with her, and she couldn't blame him. Here it was quitting time and she still had a sink full of parfait glasses and cream cups to wash, two tables in need of busing and a large carton of cosmetics to be stocked. As if that were not enough, tomorrow would be card day, the day she carefully categorized, sorted, matched and shelved eight display decks of greeting cards. She always prayed that no one would come in and order a banana split on card day, for the work was time-consuming. It was no time to be dealing with leftovers from the day before. She'd have to stay.

She telephoned Joel to say she would be late, admonished him to finish his homework, and promised a treat for dinner, then spent almost two hours hanging little plastic cases of eye shadow on metal hooks. It was nearly seven before she was done, and she still had to stop off at Edmond's grocery to pick up that something special for dinner, something special and quick. Fifteen minutes later, she started home, one large frozen deluxe pizza in tow.

She was tired, and the walk home was uphill all the way. When she reached the little clapboard house with its crooked stone chimney, she was just mechanically putting one foot in front of the other and wondering where the day had gone. She barely got through the door when Joel hit her with a barrage of loaded questions.

"Can Uncle Wes come over tomorrow? Didn't you say he could come over? Tomorrow's all right, isn't it? You haven't changed your mind, have you?"

Joy wanted to sit down and cry. She'd never felt so demoralized or fearful. Would it never end? Could it be this easy for Weston Caudell to win? If so, how long would it be before Joel came in stuttering that he wanted to live with wonderful Uncle Wes? For one awful moment she hovered on the precipice of hysterical tears, but then she thought of Cynthia and how calmly Cynthia had accepted the news that the time had come for Joy to contact her grandmother. There had been such serenity, such trust in the smile Cynthia had given her, and such affection. Well, she wasn't Cynthia, but as the beneficiary of Cynthia's wisdom, love and selflessness, she wasn't so weak and foolish as to cave in now. Summoning up all the good will, patience and faith that she had in her, she managed a small, very small, smile.

"Are you sure you want to do this?" she asked, already knowing the answer. He cocked his head at her.

"Please, Joy. You said—"

"Yes." She sighed. "Yes, I know what I said, and yes, tomorrow will be... He can come tomorrow if that's what you want."

Joel rewarded her with a rare hug and, as the young are wont to do, went instantly to another subject of intense interest.

"What's for supper? Get any pop? Pizza! All right!" Then it was into the kitchen to pull out the oven pan drawer too far and dump its contents onto the floor with clatters and pings and plunks. Joy couldn't keep from smiling at this boy, but these days even her smiles were touched by the ever-present threat of tears. Somehow, she had to get through this. And what then? Would life ever return to normal?

It was life at its most normal that got her through the next day. It was the boring, the mundane, the tedious that filled her hours and forced their passage. She kept thoughts of Weston Caudell at bay by keeping very busy and, unlike the day before, managed to get through early. She hurried home and was surprised to find that Joel had straightened the house, testament to the fact that he was nervous about this impending visit and wanted it to go well. She told herself that she must be polite to Weston Caudell for Joel's sake, but the very idea was depressing.

Forcing away the gloom, she made a hearty pot of soup from canned beans and bacon and broth and laid the table for the evening meal. Joel chattered throughout the process, telling her all about "the gang" at school, and had she heard that Old Man Monroe and Widow Grouper were getting hitched next Sunday? At their age! She lectured him absently on the proper use of the title "mister" and the disrespect inherent in such terms as "old man," and yes, she had heard and thought it rather sweet. He made a face that in other circumstances might have been associated with an upset stomach. Joy laughed, desperately needing the distraction, and went mechanically about disposing of dinner.

Joel ate heartily and kept up his chatter, apparently relaxed—until the mantel clock began to mark the appointed hour with its tinkling chime. Suddenly the easy camaraderie evaporated, leaving behind a double measure of tension. Joel himself rushed to whisk away the evidence of their shared meal and quickly retied his shoes so that one lace did not trail along inviting disaster with every step. He turned a critical eye on her.

"Get changed!" he implored. "Hurry up! He'll be here any minute!"

An intense anger swept over her. Why should she change? Who cared what Weston Caudell thought of them? But the answer was painfully obvious. Joel cared. The anger fled. Numbly, she got up and climbed the stairs. She stripped out of her working clothes and pulled on a pair of dark, clean jeans and a pale orchid sweater with a tiny satin bow at the neck and bracelet-length sleeves. She let her hair down and brushed it out, then, remembering what he had said about liking it before, she grimly swept it into a ponytail and secured it with a rubber band. It was then that she heard his knock at the door below and Joel's eager greeting as he showed him in. Weston Caudell was here. Somehow, she had to be pleasant. Defiantly, she took a moment to really study her appearance in the mirror.

She saw a small woman, a bit top-heavy perhaps, but otherwise well-proportioned, with a fresh, clean face unadorned except for a stroke of mascara on pale but thick lashes. Her skin was clear, her lips a dusty pink but in her opinion not quite full enough to achieve that sultry look women were supposed to covet, and tonight her eyes were a very vibrant blue with a touch of violet. Her hair was thick and sleek and golden blond, her best feature as far as she was concerned. All in all, she was not overjoyed with her image but, rather, was simply satisfied. It could have been worse, after all. Still, she couldn't help wondering if Weston Caudell had meant what he'd said that day beneath the tree in the churchyard.

But of course he hadn't. It was proof of how far he was willing to go to have his way. Well, if he thought compliments and flirtation were going to win her confidence, he had another think coming. She took a deep breath and went down to meet whatever lay ahead.

She could hear Joel babbling away to his guest even as she descended the stairway into the little mudroom behind the kitchen. Caudell was getting the lowdown on "old, uh, Mr. Monroe" and the Widow Grouper. Joy was a bit surprised by Caudell's comment.

"Well, just take it for testament, son, that you never get too old to need someone special in your corner."

She would have found the sentiment commendable, had it come from anyone else, and where did he get off addressing Joel with such familiarity? Well, Joel was smart enough to know he wasn't Weston Caudell's son, and eventually he was going to resent these little attempts to plant that notion—she hoped.

By the time she'd crossed the kitchen and pushed open the swinging door between that room and the living room, they'd moved on to another subject—school. Joel was naming his teachers and making comments, accompanied by descriptive faces. Weston was laughing with an understanding if not altogether approving tone.

"Mr. Caudell," she said, stepping into the room, and he came instantly to his feet, a ready smile tugging his lips into the requisite shape. Joel got up, too, his smile slightly troubled but otherwise genuine.

"Joy," Weston said, offering his hand, "or would you prefer Miss Morrow?"

She sent him a pointed glance and slid her palm over his in a semblance of a handshake. "It makes no difference," she told him icily. He bent forward in a quick bow, as if she'd paid him a lavish compliment.

"Then call me Wes, please."

Oh, he was very good. Very. She pulled herself erect. "If you insist."

"Please."

She gave him a nod, dismissing the matter, and seated herself in Cynthia's painted rocker. Wes, followed by Joel, reclaimed his seat on the sofa. For one tense moment no one said a word, then suddenly everyone was talking at once.

"Joel, why don't—"

"I appreciate—"

"Could we have—"

Then came silence again, as if a tap had been turned off, stopping the flow of words. Everyone looked away from everyone else. Wes shifted his position and crossed his legs. He was wearing corduroy slacks, and the sound generated by his action seemed ridiculously loud, but his response was an easy chuckle.

"All right, let's take turns, shall we? Ladies first."

Joy cleared her throat, disliking the way he had taken charge. "Joel, I was going to suggest that you fetch the large photo album. Maybe Mis—ah, Wes would like to see some of your pictures."

"Now that's an excellent idea," Weston put in. He tapped Joel's shoulder with the flat of his fist. "Why don't you do that?"

Joel got up immediately, obviously glad to get this visit back on track. "Sure," he said, "and after you look at the pictures, maybe we can have some refreshments. Okay, Joy?"

"We'll see," she answered stiffly. "Perhaps Wes won't want refreshments." The boy turned to him inquisitively.

"Let's decide later," he said wisely. "First let's see those pictures, but take your time. I want a word with Joy."

Her guard went up immediately, and, though his gaze was frank and his manner friendly, she allowed herself no degree of relaxation.

"Speak your mind," she bade him the moment Joel had disappeared into the tiny hallway. He spread his hands in a gesture of compliance, and because he wore the sleeves of his striped rugby shirt pushed up to the elbow, she noticed the expensive two-tone watch he wore on his wrist and the large gold-and-ruby class ring on the fourth finger of his right hand.

"I know Pritikin came to see you. I hope you won't hold his kindness to me against him. He's a good man."

"Yes, I know," she told him shortly. "Is that all?"

He tapped the fabric covering of the sofa with his forefinger. "There is one other thing," he began. "You told me not long ago that people in this town would support you. You were right."

"You've checked," she stated, folding her arms.

"I've checked," he admitted, "and I've heard only good." That sounded fine, but she wasn't willing to lower her guard just because he'd told her what she'd already known. He leaned forward, one hand going to support his chin, his elbow braced against his knee. "Joy, I know that you love Joel, and I apologize for having considered any other possibility, but now I'm asking you to consider the possibility that I might love the kid, too."

"You don't even know him," she came back smoothly, but he merely smiled.

"Joy, I know that kid like I know myself and the boy I once was. I swear, looking at him is like looking in a mirror twenty years ago." He chuckled. "Except I didn't have freckles. I was, however, small for my age and had a sweet face that made old women pinch my cheeks and the guys automatically peg me as a wimp."

"You?" she said, finding this hard to believe, but he nodded affirmatively.

"You don't know what it's like to be the runt. I mean, I grew out of it in high school, but at thirteen you think you're never going to, and it can be tough."

He seemed to know what he was talking about, but looking at him, it was hard to believe he'd ever had a moment's uncertainty. He wasn't a huge man, but he stood well over six feet, and the arms and chest bulging beneath that knit shirt were not those of a ninety-pound weakling. Still, it was possible that he had a certain empathy for his nephew. They were blood kin, after all, but the idea that they shared certain experiences troubled her, not simply because it might be true but because despite herself she was beginning to give Weston Caudell the benefit of the doubt. She felt that flutter of panic again, the same as the one she'd felt that first day when he'd walked over and introduced himself at the soda fountain. As if to show that things could, indeed, get worse, he seemed to be reading her mind.

"Anyway," he went on, "I want to apologize for being so abrupt in the beginning. It was *indelicate* of me to just announce myself without warning that day in Ball's store, but after I realized that that was Joel sitting there, I just couldn't help myself."

"You weren't waiting for him?" she queried suspiciously.

"I was," he admitted. "But I only intended to get a look at him, and size up the situation."

"You mean me. You were sizing up *me*."

"All right, I was sizing up you. You can't blame me for that, can you? I'm concerned for the boy. I have to know that whatever happens from here on, it's for *his* best."

"And if the best thing for Joel turns out to be staying here with me?" she challenged.

Weston straightened and spread his long arm along the back of the sofa. "If I decide to back off and allow Joel to stay with you," he said precisely, "and that's a big if—then it will be because you've convinced me it's the right thing to do for Joel."

She automatically bristled at the idea that he should "allow" Joel to do anything, but that "big if" was like a light at the end of a very long, very dark tunnel, and she set her sights on it with great determination. If he wanted convincing, then she was the woman for that job.

"Once you get to know me," she said, "you'll see that I'm good for your nephew. I know you're blood kin, but we're family in a way I'm not sure you can understand. We belong together, Joel and I."

He didn't seem convinced, but he didn't seem closed to the idea, either, and that was something.

"Well," he said, "that's what I'm here for, frankly—to get to know you better. You deserve to have your mind put at ease about Joel's welfare, and so do I."

She couldn't argue with that, but she just couldn't be sure about anything where Weston Caudell was concerned. He had said he wanted to be her friend, and though she didn't believe it for a minute, she had to face facts. Weston was here. He was Joel's uncle. Joel had decided he wanted to know him. She couldn't think of anything to do at the moment except play along. If in the process she could convince Weston that being with her was the best thing for Joel, it was worth whatever it took.

"You won't find me lacking as a guardian," she promised him, knowing he'd already won the first battle, and determined to win the next herself.

For a long moment his blue-grey eyes held her blue-violet ones in mysterious, careful scrutiny. Then he brought his hands together in silent emphasis.

"We'll see," he said softly. "We'll see."

Joel seemed to truly enjoy himself that evening. He and "Uncle Wes" pored over every photo album in the house and traded boyhood stories. Wes talked about his brother with an easy fondness that surprised Joy, and she realized for the first time how avid the boy was for any information about his father. Listening to the two of them talk made her feel like an outsider, but she tamped down that uncomfortable emotion and let them feed each other the knowledge they craved. After a bit, she got up and went into the kitchen to make little cheese sandwiches and triangles of cinnamon toast for snacking. It was easier, somehow, if she didn't have to listen.

Perhaps it was coincidence, or perhaps it was by design, but upon her return, Joy found them talking about movies, and Wes seemed to make a concerted effort to invite her participation. She could not deny the need to be included, but stubbornness kept her comments terse and dry, her spirits sinking more and more as Joel warmed to his uncle's charm. It was with a great sense of hope that she noticed Weston check his watch for the time.

"I have to be going soon," he said. Joy felt almost heady with relief, but Joel's obvious disappointment quickly deflated her. "But why don't we plan an outing together soon?"

Joel immediately perked up. "Yeah! Hey, great!"

Joy could only stare, appalled. "I—I don't know. We're awfully busy just now. Joel has school, and there's my job."

"We'll make it Saturday," Wes said, seizing the obvious solution.

"Where'll we go?" Joel wanted to know, his enthusiasm palpable.

"I thought I'd leave that to you and Joy."

"Oh, no," she said. "I really couldn't. I..." She couldn't think how to escape. They were staring at her.

Wes turned to Joel. "What do you say, sport? Got any ideas?"

Joel bit his lip. "Oh, boy," he said. "This is gonna be great."

In short order he laid out his idea of the perfect day. Joy made the best picnics, he said. He hadn't been up in the mountains since winter. They could hike and take the binoculars. It was gonna be great. Joy listened with dismay as the two fellows divided up the responsibilities. She, naturally, was in charge of the food. Wes claimed what he called the three B's, beverages, blankets and bug spray, while Joel received recreation as an assignment. From that point on he talked of nothing but Frisbees, bats and balls.

Shortly, Weston rose to take his leave. Joel offered him a handshake, but Wes helped himself to a hug afterward, and the boy did not object. With Joy, he confined himself to a nod, a smile and a polite thank-you. She returned the nod, still wondering how she'd gotten into this, where it would all end, how she was going to make it through the next meeting—and the next and... Dear God, what had she let herself in for? Suddenly it was brought home to her just how dangerous a man Weston Caudell really was. She promised herself as the door closed on his back that she would not forget.

Saturday was bright and golden with that diaphanous sunlight peculiar to spring. Even indoors Joy could feel the sunshine on her skin like gossamer, weightless and cool but silky and somehow substantial. Spring itself seemed perched on the very brink of full bloom, as if at any moment the flowers would burst with brilliant petals and new leaves would mature to full size and color. The day seemed made for a picnic, but it was only with reluctance that Joy got up and drew her bath.

She dressed in comfortable jeans and a pink T-shirt worn beneath a long-sleeved shirt of blue and pink and purple plaid, which she tied at her waist. Next, more to kill time than for any other reason, she plaited a pink ribbon into her hair so that a loose braid lay against the back of her head and hung down between her shoulder blades, tied at the end with a soft bow. Then, unable to put off the inevitable any longer, she went downstairs to make breakfast and pack a basket.

In the kitchen, however, she found Joel already munching a bowl of cold cereal, which shot breakfast as she didn't like to cook only for herself. She had to be content with a couple of pieces of toast and a cup of weak coffee. Afterward, with Joel's prompting, she began to prepare the picnic.

Joel talked a mile a minute while she fried up chicken and stirred together a potato salad from ingredients prepared the evening before. Wasn't Uncle Wes pretty neat? he wanted to know. A picnic was a super idea. He bet Uncle Wes would bring pop to drink. It was a shame they couldn't take the freezer and make some ice cream. Did she figure Uncle Wes could play softball? Bet he could. It would be fun to use the binoculars. No telling how many birds and critters they could spot. And how about some sweet pickles?

She ignored as many of his questions as she could, but when he got to the pickles, she went immediately to the refrigerator and took out the jar, then began to slice a ripe red tomato into hefty chunks.

A cucumber followed the tomato, and a bunch of tiny green onions, then a wedge of sharp cheddar and a half-dozen hard-boiled eggs. She supplemented this bounty with apples, a fresh loaf of white bread, a small pot each of margarine and honey, and finally, a feather-light sponge cake cut into great, airy pieces. As an afterthought, she tossed in a bag of plump marshmallows. She hardly had the basket packed when Weston arrived. He was driving a Chevrolet Suburban so new it still had plastic on its seats and a sticker on the window.

He and Joel loaded the picnic gear into the vehicle, Joel discovering a highly polished acoustic guitar stowed behind the back seat. Wes told him he could play with it on the way up the mountain if he was careful, and Joel settled right down in the back seat with the instrument on his lap, leaving Joy to occupy the wide front seat with Weston.

They drove up the mountain and at Joel's direction turned off on a narrow, rutted track that wound around rocky outcroppings and clumps of trees to a small, deep-blue lake, beside which they halted and spread out their gear in the shade. Weston was being pleasant but a little aloof, which made it easier for Joy to be pleasant. With Joel, he was so very relaxed, so very easy that the two of them might have known each other a lifetime, and while that did not thrill her, she had to give a little credit where credit was due. Weston knew how to conduct himself. There could be no doubt about that.

The hours before lunchtime were filled with a game of Bat the Ball, the three of them taking turns in each position. Weston proved particularly adept at pitching, but neither Joel nor Joy were any real competition in any area. Wes promised to teach Joel a thing or two about batting and fielding, and Joy found it rather cheeky of him. But Joel, of course, was delighted.

Disgruntled, Joy went to lay out their lunch. After a few moments she became aware of the resonant hum of the guitar. Wes was teaching Joel a few simple chords that, when put together properly, turned out to be a real song. She paused to watch as Joel strummed through it. The boy beamed, the ease of the exercise a natural ego builder. Again Joy could not help noting how well Wes seemed to handle him.

"Lunch," she called, and the guitar was set aside.

The pair of them fell upon her prepared feast like starving peasants, snatching choice tidbits and stuffing themselves without compunction. Joy let them gorge, pleased despite herself. Afterward, Joel lay back on the red felt blanket provided by Wes and promptly started to snore. Wes chuckled silently, then turned away to help Joy clean up after their meal. She tried to tell him it wasn't necessary, whispering and mouthing her message, but he merely smiled and kept folding things and putting on lids, finally stretching out his hand to place a forefinger against her moving lips. The effect was particularly quelling, as his touch seemed to carry a small electrical charge that made her lip tingle for long moments afterward. She immediately looked away, disturbed once more, but in a new and unfamiliar way.

The leftovers packed away, Wes quietly took up his guitar, stretched out between Joel and Joy, his back to a tree trunk, and began to strum softly. The tune had a mournful quality to it, a dreamy, lilting, fluid cadence that made her think of Spanish ballads and pianos. She sat very still, painfully aware of the man next to her, and stared up into the mottled ceiling of the treetops. She tried not to let it affect her, but the music began to work a strange magic, conjuring up candlelit images of wineglasses and snowy-white table linen spread for two, of hands twined beneath the table and long, lingering looks. After a bit, the boy stirred and struggled up on his elbows, blinking. Almost at once, Joel pointed to a branch across the way.

"Hey, get the binoculars," he whispered rapidly. "I think I've spotted a woodpecker over there." Wes set aside the guitar and went quietly to the truck to do as Joel asked. He came back quickly, the cheap binoculars in tow, and the boy took them, training them on the spot where he thought a yellow-crowned bird perched. After a while he put them down and shook his head. "Naw. Guess I was dreaming."

"Let me look," Wes urged, and the boy handed over the glasses. Wes took a long time adjusting the focus. "Well, there's something in that tree," he pronounced at length. "It's hard to tell what with these glasses, but maybe if we get closer..." He and Joel quietly got to their feet, and Joel started away in a stalker's crouch, but Wes lingered a moment, looking down at Joy. "Coming?" She shook her head. "Aw, come on. Don't you want to see what we find?"

"I'll wait," she said, leaning on her elbows, and he smiled down at her, dropping a hand to her shoulder. It was only a mindless gesture, but an odd warmth seemed to radiate from that hand, flowing throughout her body. Then it was gone as Wes quickly followed his nephew.

Joy was, in fact, glad for the respite. She was all too aware of Weston Caudell, not that she considered this unusual. They were, after all, combatants in a certain sense. It was natural to be on edge around the competition. She wished he would be a bit more circumspect about touching her, however. It made her feel... vulnerable.

She got up straight away and went down to the lake's edge and started skipping stones across its blue surface. Her precious moments of solitude lengthened to a long while. And she became so intent upon her activity that she didn't hear her companions return.

They crept up on her in silent conspiracy, Joel with his binoculars in his hands, Wes with a wicked gleam in his eyes, and just as she drew back her arm to throw the smooth stone in her hand, they pounced, Joel screeching like a banshee, Wes poking quick fingers into her ribs. Joy screamed and faltered, the motion of her arm carrying her forward toward the water's edge. She was but an instant from dunking herself in the icy lake when strong arms caught her about the waist and hauled her backward, their owner laughing into her ear.

"What do you think you're doing?" she howled once she'd regained her footing. "Let go!" She swung her elbows, clearing a space for herself within the confines of his arms.

"All right," Wes was saying. "It was just a joke."

"A joke!" she spat. "A joke is funny. You nearly scared the wits out of me!"

"Boy, I thought you were gonna jump in the lake," Joel giggled, immediately soothing Joy's temper. She realized with some relief that he didn't realize how angry she was.

"No, I wasn't going to jump in the lake," she assured him as lightly as she could. "I was going to fight. You're lucky I didn't throw you in."

"Ho, I'm scared!" Joel teased. He held the binoculars between his knees, stuck his fingers in his ears, crossed his eyes and wiggled his tongue. Joy felt her anger quickly evolving into indulgent humor, and latched on to the new feeling as a means by which to switch her focus entirely to Joel. She'd show the little scamp, she decided, suddenly darting toward him, but he was prepared for this very thing and took off. He was fast, and Wes slowed her a bit by trying to catch her in his arms, but even at that she caught up with Joel after a few yards, pulling just close enough to get a hold on his shirt tail. She dug in her feet, effectively throwing the boy off balance. He went tumbling to the ground, kicking out harmlessly and laughing even before she fell on him, her fingers tickling the sensitive flesh covering his ribs.

"Help!" he gasped. "Uncle Wes! Help!"

She tried to retreat, realizing too late that by playing their game she'd left herself open to a full press. Wes came in laughing, squatted and gently pushed her aside, then reached out and locked his arms around her as if she might resist after all and go after the boy. She had no such intention, but Joel couldn't have known that. He was up in a flash and launching himself into them. Suddenly they were rolling, all three of them together, across the ground, a mass of knees and elbows and flailing limbs. Joy yelped, while Weston laughed into her ear and Joel shouted playfully that he was going to get her. Then she felt herself lifted and rolled again, and the next instant she was looking up into the sheepish face of Weston Caudell. His hair had fallen forward, and he was smiling anxiously, Joel peering over his right shoulder like a curious puppy.

For a moment all was silent. Then Joel began to laugh. "No fair," he said. "You're supposed to be helping me."

Those smoky-blue eyes pulled away from hers. "Who said?" He turned on his elbow, his forearm flexing beneath her shoulders, and he and Joel laughed together.

Joy quickly twisted away, raising herself up into a sitting position, leaves and twigs dangling from wisps of her hair. Weston slowly sat up. Joel sank down onto his heels, wagging a finger at her.

"We got you good," he teased, and she managed a limp smile, feeling heat spread through her cheeks.

"You sneak," she said, her voice trembling despite its lightness.

"Oh, man, I need a drink," Wes said loudly, and he cuffed Joel affectionately on the jaw. "How about it, sport? You started this, I vote you get the pop."

Joel got up, grinning from ear to ear. "All right. All right. Boy, Joy," he said, brushing dust from his pants, "you're fast."

She merely smiled as he moved away, avoiding Weston's gaze. Weston dusted off his shoulders, silent as Joel moved toward the picnic site. After a moment he drew up his legs and folded them Indian style.

"Sorry about that," he said softly, and she sent him a sharp glance.

"Nothing's broken."

"It wasn't my idea."

"Forget it," she told him, and struggled to her feet. He caught her wrist in his hand, his gaze direct, almost pleading.

"I'm not a monster," he said. "I'm just a man who wants to know his nephew."

"Just to know him?" she asked. "Not to *have* him?"

He seemed to think about that, his eyes leaving her face and coming back again. "I don't want to hurt you," he said. "That's not my purpose at all." It wasn't exactly a clear-cut answer, but the scuffing of footsteps in the dirt and the clinking of bottles precluded further discussion. Joy pulled her hand away, thinking it was just as well. How could she believe him, whatever he might say? She smiled and smoothed her hair, lifting a hand to receive the bottle of pop Joel carried forward.

While they drank, Joel told her what they'd spied through the binoculars. It didn't amount to much, a squirrel and a wren and a wood mouse, but then what could one expect from such an inferior pair of binoculars? Uncle Wes, it seemed, had promised him a better pair, if that was all right with her.

"Uncle Wes is very generous," she mumbled noncommittally, "but I think we'd better be heading home now."

Slowly Wes got up, and they turned toward the vehicle parked beside the tree. Before long they were packed up and ready to roll. They piled into the truck for the return trip, Joy claiming the back seat for herself this time. Wes reached for the key in the ignition, then halted.

"I've meant to tell you," he said, sitting back and spreading his arm along the back of the seat. "I'm taking a house in town."

"No kidding?" Joel erupted. "That's great!"

But it was Joy to whom Weston looked, turning his head and twisting about to face her over his shoulder. She stared at him, appalled by what seemed a most ominous revelation, but then he did a most peculiar thing. He reached over the seat and took her hand, as if to reassure her.

She was too stunned to do or say anything. Those gray-blue eyes held hers, and his fingers coiled tightly about her own. Then he released her and withdrew his arm. An instant later, she turned to stare unseeingly through the window, and the engine rumbled to life beneath the hood of the vehicle.

He was staying, she told herself as they bounced over the rutted track back toward the road. Weston Caudell was staying in Folly Creek, and life was never going to be the same again.

Chapter Four

She had no idea how much Weston's actual residence in Folly Creek would affect their lives. Not only did he continue to show up at the little church on the mountain, he became an active member, much to Pritikin Marsh's delight. Next he joined the Chamber of Commerce, calling himself a private financial manager, and soon thereafter he began to show up routinely at weekly town meetings. Then one day Joel came home from school to announce excitedly that Uncle Wes was going to speak to the student body on Career Day, and shortly after that it was printed in the *Folly Creek Crier* that Weston Caudell, having taken the community to his heart, had made a large contribution to the local library. All at once Weston Caudell was not only an accepted part of the community but a celebrated one. It seemed to Joy that he had done everything in his power to ingratiate himself with the local populace, and she was not pleased, for as Weston's influence grew, hers diminished, at least so far as community support went.

Joel, however, seemed ecstatic. Everywhere he went people were talking about his Uncle Wes and telling him what a lucky boy he was to have such a generous fellow in the family. Joy felt powerless to do anything to blunt the force of Weston's growing popularity. If she complained or displayed suspicion, people would undoubtedly see that as jealousy and fear, which it was. Moreover, she had no means by which to compete. No one wanted a glorified soda jerk to encourage students to follow in her footsteps, and as far as the library was concerned, she couldn't even afford to pay overdue book fines let alone make huge contributions. She had no choice but to swallow her pride, smile and keep her suspicions of ulterior motives to herself.

Ironically, Weston's polite attentiveness did nothing to win her trust. He made a point of including her in every outing to which he treated Joel. He asked her permission before he presented the boy with a gift and her advice before he purchased it. He brought dessert when invited to dinner—after much wheedling on Joel's part—and reciprocated with an expensive restaurant meal Joy could not hope to match. And he made a point of deferring to her authority in all things concerning his nephew. Joy had no choice but to meet him smile for smile, invitation for invitation, compliment for compliment, deference for deference, at least publicly, but she knew without qualification that she couldn't hope to beat him at his own game.

The longer this game of civility went on, the greater the tension grew between them, and yet Joy somehow managed to maintain her obsequious behavior, while Weston gradually insinuated himself into every area of their lives. Once, he even offered to go over their finances and help them plan a new budget. Joy had to get a grip on her temper before she could point out that their budget consisted entirely of utility payments, groceries, modest contributions to the church, a small allowance for Joel and a very conservative savings program aimed at covering emergencies and property taxes and an occasional treat. It was not, she pointed out, as if there were really any options, at which point he offered to help out with expenses. She turned him down firmly, being wise enough to realize that contributing to Joel's support would serve to strengthen his case for guardianship.

The ease with which Weston Caudell spent money was particularly galling, and the more so as Joel's birthday drew near. Joy dipped into her savings to buy him an expensive wrist watch and made a list of friends to invite over for cake and ice cream. Wes, however, insisted on hosting the party, and they argued about it. Joy intended to sponsor the party herself, but after a good bit of wrangling Weston did manage to convince her to compromise. Almost as soon as she agreed to share the planning and expense with him, she regretted it. They argued over everything, and to her dismay Joy realized that more often than not, Wes came out the winner. Suddenly the small reception she'd envisioned had turned into a real event with a guest list much too large to be accommodated by her tiny house. There was nothing to do except turn the whole thing over to Weston, for to do anything else, to have cut back or canceled, would have disappointed Joel deeply.

Even Wes's big rented house could not contain the party. On the appointed evening people spilled out onto the wide porches, with grilled hamburgers on paper plates and cups of pop in their hands. It was, indeed, some shindig. The whole town was there, reveling in Weston Caudell's generosity. Wes took up his guitar and joined a fiddle player and a banjo picker in one corner of the wide veranda to provide some real foot-stomping music while various others supplied the occasional vocals. Meanwhile the outdoor activities were organized into games of tetherball, tug-o'-war, horseshoes and three-tag tag.

Joy somehow got the role of hostess, and she couldn't help resenting having so much responsibility dumped on her when the whole thing had been Wes's idea. While he wowed the townsfolk with his guitar strumming and his generosity, Joy kept busy directing traffic to one of the three bathrooms in the great stone house, filling cups with pop, mopping up the inevitable spills and answering endless questions. In fact, she was working so hard at fulfilling her assumed chores that she didn't even notice when Wes handed over his instrument to another player and systematically went about piling two plates with hamburgers, salad, chips and baked beans, so that when he showed up at her elbow and smilingly demanded she hold them, she complied without really understanding what was going on. It wasn't until he returned with two large cups of soda, traded her a drink for a plate, and ordered her to follow him that she realized she'd just been given her dinner.

"This is a party, you know," he told her as he picked a spot on the porch railing and leaned against it. He steadied his cup on the three-inch wide railing and took up his fork with his free hand. "Relax."

"That's easy for you to say," she sniffed. "You've been acting like a guest at your own party."

His mouth was full of beans, but he quickly dispensed with them. "That's the key to throwing a good party," he told her. "I like parties that just sort of manage themselves, you know?"

"No," she muttered, picking at her salad. "I'm afraid I don't."

He chuckled. "You sound like my father. He seems to think a party is an exercise in martyrdom. The man isn't happy unless he's unhappy, you know?" Joy shook her head, chewing a chunk of tomato. He popped a chip into his mouth, chewed and swallowed. "My parents are fond of saying that great wealth brings great responsibility, which, I confess, is probably correct. But—they seem to feel that the greatest of the great responsibilities is protecting the social position that comes with it. Consequently they don't enjoy their money very much. They maintain this great mausoleum of an ancestral home, only it's not a home; it's just this great big house where everyone speaks civilly to one another about things that don't matter and never, ever, discuss the things that do."

This was a surprising revelation made all the more so by the calm, accepted manner in which it was delivered. It was not, she noted, resignation but rather understanding, and it cast a fresh light not only on what she knew about his parents but also what she knew about him. She put her fork down and picked up her hamburger, suddenly hungry.

"What does this have to do with their feelings about Cynthia and Joel?"

He thought that over while he finished off his beans. "Well, see, it's like this in their minds: only a person born to money can rightly understand the duty connected with it. Now you take someone who's never had two nickels to rub together, load 'em up with cold hard cash, and it's going to be spend, spend, spend, without an inkling as to tradition or duty. According to my father, the problem is a crass attitude, a coarse tendency to focus entirely on one's primitive desires. Apparently it has to be eliminated from one's ancestral line by generations of careful breeding."

"So Cynthia's pedigree didn't measure up," she said. He nodded his head. Joy was so appalled she lost her appetite and put her burger back on the plate. "That's the most snobbish thing I've ever heard."

He smiled at her, his own burger in his hand. "Well, you have to remember how they were raised themselves."

Joy stared at him, trying to correctly gauge his opinion of his parents' attitude. "You don't agree with them, do you?"

He seemed about to answer her, then someone hailed him from across the way, snagging his attention. He put down his burger and lifted his hand in greeting, then took up his cup. He turned back to Joy, his gaze flat and level. "What do you think?"

She stared at him, wondering what she did think and what it was he expected her to say. Finally, she shrugged. "I don't know."

He just looked at her. "You don't know," he said. "Despite the fact that I'm here at Joel's birthday party in my house in his town, that I've bent over backward—" He broke off and looked for a moment at his plate. "I'm a lot of things," he said slowly, "but I am not a snob."

"Just saying it doesn't make it so," she muttered.

He opened his mouth as if to speak again, but seemed to think better of it and dropped his gaze. He stood there a moment, staring at his plate, then shook his head, turned and walked away.

She felt like a heel, knowing she'd insulted him and, worse yet, that she'd meant to. But how was she supposed to know one way or another how his mind worked? Just because he'd taken the town by storm, turned Joel's head, impressed the preacher... A sense of guilt swamped her, but she didn't go after him, didn't apologize, didn't even acknowledge that she understood his feelings had been hurt. Instead she made herself busy, playing hostess without complaint for the remainder of the evening, then staying behind to help clean up, even though Weston himself went to bed, apparently content to leave the cleaning to the temporary hired help.

She felt completely unappreciated, knowing that this, too, was the product of a guilty conscience, and went home in a sulk. The next day, after a fitful night's sleep, she baked a loaf of pumpkin bread, wrapped it and wrote out a formal note of thanks for the party, then called Joel home from a friend's house and firmly instructed him that he was to deliver the packet along with a personal thank-you. He went off on his bike to make the delivery and returned an hour later to say that Weston thanked her for the thank-you and would be joining them for dinner! That was a piece of news that piqued Joy greatly, a guilty conscience being a handy irritant. Who did he think he was, inviting himself over for dinner like that?

Nevertheless, he did come for dinner, and she did go to extra lengths to be pleasant. She baked a chicken nestled among potatoes and carrots, and stewed a pot of peas, and she put a cloth over the table and got out the embroidered napkins Cynthia had received as a wedding gift. She made sure all of the flatware matched, which wasn't difficult for three place settings but would have been impossible for four, and got out the pretty hand-painted rose glasses Cynthia had collected through a promotion at Edmond's Grocery.

Her efforts seemed to pay off. Weston was his usual self. Not a mention was made of that unfortunate conversation, and both he and Joel were effusively complimentary of the meal. They talked and joked together, and each made an effort to include her in the conversation. Afterward, at Wes's insistence, they all cleaned up, forming a kind of production line with Wes washing, Joel rinsing and Joy drying and putting away. It was a much more relaxed time than Joy had envisioned, and she could only wonder how he managed to pretend as if he hadn't been insulted by her reluctance to credit him with a lack of snobbery. He was a difficult man to figure, this Weston Caudell.

She put the last dish into the cabinet and closed the door while Wes and Joel finished going over the stove top. There was something satisfying about being done with an especially good meal, and she was feeling particularly well just then for some reason. Life felt oddly safe at the moment. It was a nostalgic feeling, and it seemed to her for a little while as if Cynthia had never climbed that ladder, as if she were in the next room, humming some little song to herself and shuffling the cards for a game. Joy was just about to suggest a few hands of gin rummy, thinking how like old times it would be with three of them playing, when Joel glanced at his new wrist watch and announced that he was late.

"Late?" Joy echoed. "What could you be late for?"

"It's Sean," Joel told her plaintively. "We were playing chess before, only we didn't get to finish, remember? And I promised I'd go back after dinner to finish the game. Please, Joy? I'm ahead and everything."

"But you have company," she reminded him, only to have Weston contradict her.

"An uncle's not company, he's family."

She sent Wes a killing glance and turned her attention back to the boy. "I think you should stay home."

"Please, Joy," the boy pleaded. "Uncle Wes doesn't mind."

Joy looked to Weston, expecting him to recant now that he knew where she stood on the matter. Instead, he leaned against the edge of the kitchen counter and folded his arms as if to say, "Play the ogre by yourself, kiddo." She glared at him momentarily, but there was a decision to be made and she was the one to make it. She bit her cheek, pondering, but was unable for some reason to form a coherent thought. Finally, she threw up her hands in surrender.

"Oh, all right. But next time, young man, you check your plans out with me first, got it?"

"I will," he promised, already heading for the door. "Thanks, Joy."

"Knock him off the board, champ," Wes told him as he let himself out.

"And be back here by nine o'clock," Joy called after him, "whether you've beaten him by then or not!"

The screen door banged shut in the mudroom, and a moment later Joel whizzed by the window on his bike. It occurred to her that this whole thing was her fault. If she hadn't insulted Weston before, if she hadn't felt so guilty, if she hadn't called Joel away from Sean's to deliver the message, if she hadn't let Weston bulldoze his way in here... Her good mood had vanished. She slapped the countertop with the damp dishcloth still in her hand.

Weston smiled and scratched an ear. "Well, I guess Joel's finally had it with all this adult attention."

She merely glowered.

"I think it's encouraging," he went on. "I mean, we want him to pal around with his friends like any other normal boy, don't we?"

"Yes," she agreed. "Certainly."

They stood there a moment, an awkward silence enveloping them. Then Weston smiled, and Joy tried to do likewise, managing only to grimace.

"Don't feel you have to stay," she told him stiffly. "You're probably wanting to go home."

"I don't want to go home," he said, stepping forward, and then he reached out and took the dishcloth from her.

It seemed an odd thing to do, taking the dishcloth like that, and she looked at him, watching as he tossed it away. Still, she had no idea what was coming until he literally took her in his arms, and even then she was too slow catching on to do anything about it. Almost before she could think, his mouth covered hers, his arms pulling her close. Stunned, she just stood there, feeling herself gathered against him, his mouth moving over hers, coaxing, experimenting. Numbed by the shock of it, she felt nothing at first, then heat flashed through her, exploding the nerve endings in her body in ripples like strings of firecrackers.

Suddenly her skin felt hypersensitized, bringing a new awareness of all that was happening and all that surrounded her. The cool spring breeze contrasted sharply with the warmth of his body pressed to hers. His arms were heavy about her, his chin sharp against her jaw. The breath from his nostrils was moist and hot upon her cheek. His mouth seemed incredibly soft yet strong, manipulating hers with skill and ease.

She didn't even think of resisting him, but neither did she think of joining him. It was happening to her, and yet she was apart from it. It was like living in some strange extra dimension, there and yet not there, experiencing and observing at the same time. Yet somewhere deep inside her a war was being waged, the issue still ill defined, until slowly it coalesced. The issue was sincerity. Did he mean this as a weapon by which to control her, bend her to his will? She knew suddenly that she dared not believe otherwise.

Anger swelled in her, and sadness crowded out the pleasure of being held in his arms and having his mouth against hers. She realized abruptly how very pleasurable it was, how deeply she resented being the means to the end rather than the end itself. It occurred to her, standing there within the circle of Weston's arms, her head bent beneath his, that Joel was perhaps the only person on the face of the earth who loved her simply for herself. That thought proved the catalyst she needed to remove herself from Weston Caudell's arms. She wedged her hands against the wall of his chest and pushed.

Wes loosened his embrace and slowly lifted his mouth. Joy stood stiffly, her jaw set, eyes narrowed. Wes dropped his arms and stepped away, a look of disappointment overtaking his face.

"Okay," he said, blowing out a pent-up breath, "maybe it was a bad idea."

"Maybe?" she asked archly. He looked wounded, his face tensing before he turned his gaze away. She felt a sharp stab of some emotion she dared not name, but the next moment he turned back, his eyes so steely and cold that she forgot about it altogether.

He folded his arms and struck a casual pose. "Is there a man I don't know about?"

"No man," she told him evenly.

"Don't you like men?" The tone was acerbic, angry. She widened her blue eyes.

"*Some* men."

"But not me."

"I didn't say that."

"You didn't have to."

"Think what you want," she retorted sharply, and the whole situation deteriorated into a full-blown fight.

"What am I supposed to think?" Wes shouted. "Maybe you just don't like grown men. Maybe you like them young enough so you can control them."

It was an obvious reference to Joel, and it was ugly. They glared at one another, then suddenly he stalked to the door, pushed it open, and looked at her.

"Tell me something," he said. "Joel will be a man some day, his own man. What will you do then? Who will you have then?"

She stared at him, telling herself he was the vilest thing ever to walk the earth, the meanest, the most manipulative—and yet, when he stepped through the door and let it swing closed behind him, she began to cry, another part of her longing that it not be so, and yet another disbelieving it. She heard the slight rasp of his footsteps across the living-room floor, followed by the slow creak of the front door and the bump as it closed again.

"I'll have Joel," she said to his unhearing ears. "I'll always have Joel. You can't take him away from me. You can't." But her own words came back to haunt her. *Just saying it doesn't make it so.*

Joel put down the telephone receiver and frowned. "You don't reckon he's mad at me, do you?"

Joy chose her words carefully, sensing the depth of his disappointment. Numerous calls had resulted only in a lot of ringing—and a very long, sad face. "I can't imagine why he'd be angry at you," she said soothingly. "You have to remember that he does have a life of his own to live."

"Yeah, I guess so." He walked over to the couch, slumping, and flopped down, his dirty sneakers flying up to land on the edge of the little coffee table.

Joy flipped through her magazine, pretending to be absorbed. "Joel," she went on, keeping her tone light, "has it occurred to you that one day your Uncle Wes might want to move away from here?" She glanced up to a face clouded with worried concern.

"He say that to you?"

"No," she admitted quickly. "Not in so many words."

"He wouldn't do it," the boy stated firmly, looking at his toes. "He wouldn't, Joy. He told me. He said if I wanted him to stay here he would."

She looked back at her magazine, stung with jealousy. "I see." She turned the page. "I didn't realize you'd discussed it."

"Yeah, you know, it came up."

"What if he did go away?" she pressed, lowering the magazine when he didn't answer right away. He was biting his bottom lip, his eyebrows pulled into a frown.

"I'd probably write to him, I guess," he said at last. She nodded, relieved in a way.

"Well, never you mind," she told him gently. "It doesn't bear thinking about. You've always got me."

He smiled lamely and sat up, his feet dropping to the floor. "I guess I should have stayed home last night. It was rude of me to go to Sean's while Uncle Wes was here, wasn't it?"

She closed the magazine and tossed it onto the table, leaning forward in the rocker, her elbows upon her knees, hands clasped. "You're not a rude boy," she said. "Don't worry. He'll be back. I know it. But, Joel, don't you think you're getting a bit too involved? We really don't know him very well yet. Give it time, okay?"

He looked at her for a moment, then shrugged his shoulders. "Guess I'll go to bed."

She nodded and glumly watched him get to his feet and shuffle across the room. "Good night," she said as he turned into the hallway. "Sweet dreams."

He murmured a lackluster reply and disappeared. Joy put her hands to her head. Damn Weston Caudell. Why did he have to come here? Was there nothing she could do to get him out of their lives? She knew the answer to that well enough. She'd given it plenty of thought during the past twenty-four hours, and whatever fantasies she might have entertained during the wee hours of the morning, Joel had banished a minute ago. She couldn't just tell him his saintly uncle was a manipulative cad. In his current state, he wouldn't believe her, and if she proved it to him she'd only succeed in breaking his heart. He'd had enough of that.

It was simply a matter of waiting it out, she told herself, and whatever happened, she and Joel would be together. And as long as they were together, they would be fine.

She had to believe that. She had to.

For Joel's sake, she said nothing about that kiss, not to Joel and not to Weston when he finally came around again after a two-day absence, murmuring excuses about sudden business crises. Yet she couldn't behave as if nothing had happened, and neither, apparently, could Wes. In the beginning their conversation consisted of short phrases and monosyllabic replies, which they both tried to augment with chatty comments to Joel. Gradually even that deteriorated, and their talk became that of double entendres and curt, thinly veiled references. Joel, of course, was bright enough to know there had been some sort of disagreement, and he quite naturally assumed that he was the cause. It was during their third meeting after the kiss that he finally just asked right out what had gone wrong.

It was a Saturday, and the church staff had scheduled a work day in order to paint walls and make minor repairs around the building. Much to Joy's obvious disgust, she, Joel and Weston were all assigned painting jobs saving those volunteers with more expertise for the more complicated matters. They were working alone together on the very last room, a Sunday School classroom only slightly larger than the average closet. It was inevitable that they would get in one another's way. Wes tried to minimize the inconvenience by organizing the effort: he assigned himself the ceiling and the uppermost portion of the walls, Joy got the woodwork and the lower section, while Joel received the easily reachable middle. Everyone worked in a different area, so that in short order all four walls and the ceiling were in various stages of completion. Nevertheless, there was the occasional splatter and overlap, and it wasn't very long before every one of them had paint on their skin and clothes and in their hair.

Then, just as it all seemed to be coming together, Joy backed up toward the center of the little room to gauge the progress only to find herself involved in a collision. It was just a bump really, but it knocked the brush out of her hand and onto her foot. She glared at Weston, who glared back. Paint had sloshed out of the can he was carrying and onto his leg in a long, white streak. She snapped at him without thinking.

"Can't you watch where you're going?"

"Me? I'm not the idiot who was walking backward in a room full of paint. *I* was working."

"Holding a pail is not working, and I wouldn't put it past you to stand in my way intentionally!"

Weston opened his mouth to retort, but just then Joel, who had been listening to the whole thing, dropped his roller, marched forward and pushed his way between them.

"Cut it out!"

Coming from Joel, the order was doubly arresting. Wes stopped, his form frozen. Joy, too, was instantly hushed, her attention abruptly switching to the boy. They had been conducting open warfare, and the realization of it heightened the color in Joy's cheeks. Wes put a hand over his mouth in what seemed an unconscious expression of the same idea.

"You're acting like two-year-olds," Joel informed them, and Joy couldn't help shooting a resentful, accusatory glance in Weston's direction, only to find him firing back one of his own. The boy crossed his arms, assuming the role of adult as if to emphasize their childishness. "All right," he said, "I want to know what's happened. You've been downright nasty to one another for days." He looked from one to the other, obviously awaiting an answer.

Joy took a deep breath. "I don't know what you mean," she began, but the boy's face suddenly contorted into the kind of grimace that often precedes tears.

She and Wes once again exchanged loaded glances, and this time the concern was all for the boy.

Wes spread his hands. "You're right," he said, facing the boy squarely. "We had an argument, Joy and I."

Joel dropped his head, his foot scuffing the newspaper covering the floor. "I knew it," he muttered, and the eyes he raised to them were filled with pain. "It was about me, wasn't it?"

"No!" They gave him the answer in unison, each a bit surprised to find the other in agreement. Joy swallowed a lump in her throat.

"It wasn't about you. It—it wasn't about anything, really. It was just one of those silly things that got blown out of proportion, wasn't it, Wes?" She looked hopefully to Weston for corroboration.

Weston stooped to set down the gallon can of paint and straightened again, raising a spattered hand to scratch his ear. "Actually," he said, "it was something that I did—and Joy had every reason to be upset with me."

Joy's mouth came open, and her head nearly fell off her neck.

"What did you do?" Joel wanted to know, and Joy immediately launched a series of coughs, hoping to deflect attention.

Wes answered grimly. "Something stupid," he said, "and since it has nothing whatsoever to do with you, I hope you'll understand if I don't want to talk about it."

Joy took a deep breath, winding down the cough, and surreptitiously watched Joel's reaction. He seemed to think a moment, then simply shrugged.

"I just want you to quit fighting," he said. "I want us to be friends, all of us."

Well, it was out of the question, of course. She twisted around, leaving the obvious unsaid, and encountered Wes with an expectant look upon his face.

"How about it, Joy?" he said slowly. "Are you ready to bury the hatchet?"

Yeah, she thought, *right in your head.* It was, after all, his fault, just as he'd said. But Joel was standing there waiting for her to say that all was forgiven, and she couldn't very well refuse a peace offering without getting into why she couldn't trust the man. As usual, since the moment Weston Caudell had appeared, she found that she didn't have much choice except to go along. She squared her shoulders, accepting the inevitable.

"I can forget it if you can."

For a long moment Weston said nothing, then he gently shook his head. "I don't know about that," he told her quietly, "but if it helps to say I'm sorry..."

She didn't know how to reply to that or what to think of it, so she merely nodded, muttering, "All right."

Joel wiped his hands together as if he'd just done a full day's work. "Well, that takes care of that," he said. "Now, can we finish up, please? I don't want to spend the whole weekend here."

Weston cuffed him playfully and told him to get back on the end of that roller if he wanted to get the job done, then bent and picked up Joy's brush for her. She took it from him without quite meeting his eyes. He could apologize all he wanted, but it didn't change anything. They were not friends. They weren't going to be friends, and nothing could change that. Nothing. Absolutely.

Chapter Five

Joel would not leave it alone. It was not enough that his uncle wanted to endlessly entertain him, Joy had to be along to witness it. She knew it wasn't really like that. She knew she should be grateful that he tried so hard to include her, that he wanted her along, but Weston Caudell's mere presence put her teeth on edge, and worse yet, she couldn't even show it. Goodness no. She couldn't upset the boy. She couldn't speak her mind, sound like a jealous, suspicious harridan, not with saintly Uncle Wes there for comparison. She tried to convince him she was too tired to go.

"Does anyone recall that I worked all day? My feet hurt and my hands are chapped."

"What do chapped hands have to do with going for ice cream?" Wes wanted to know.

Joy glowered at him. "My hands are chapped from dipping ice cream and washing up after it's melted all over everything."

"Ah. And I suppose Ball doesn't carry a reputable hand cream in that store of his?"

"Very funny."

Joel screwed up his face. "Come on, Joy. Your hands look fine to me, and you can put your feet up in the booth. It just wouldn't be the same without you."

She sighed, irritated and defeated. "All right, if you insist."

But in the days to follow, she was to hear that same refrain over and over again. "Come with us, Joy. It wouldn't be the same without you." The movies, it seemed, wouldn't be the same without her. A hike through the woods wouldn't be the same without her. Fishing wouldn't be the same without her. She tried to tell him that Wes might want it to be just guys more often, but he said something about the Three Musketeers and how they were a kind of team, a unit.

"Besides," he told her, "Wes likes you. He likes you a lot. You know he does."

Joy looked at him thoughtfully, wondering exactly what had convinced him of this. Had he somehow learned of that ridiculous kiss? If so, Wes had to have told him, but surely he wouldn't have done such a thing. Surely Wes knew better than to talk about... well, private matters to an impressionable thirteen-year-old boy. Or did he? Exasperated, she decided she could never be certain just what that man was going to do.

Perhaps it wasn't such a good idea for him and Joel to spend time alone together after all. Perhaps she ought to speak to Weston Caudell about what the proper topics might be—and not be—for discussion with an adolescent boy. Then again, why open herself up to a discussion of...?

Her cheeks pinked every time she thought about that kiss, even when there was no one to see. She decided to let matters ride. Why stir up a hornet's nest? Doing nothing was becoming a habit where Weston Caudell was concerned, but how could she take action when she never knew what action was best to take?

It might have been easier if Wes hadn't been on his best behavior, but ever since the apology, he'd comported himself like a perfect gentleman. He seemed to make a point of holding doors for her, inquiring about her preferences and comfort, even complimenting her. She felt like escorted royalty when they went to the theater, and when they went hiking into the woods to see the wakening redbuds, he displayed such a concern for her safety that he kept her hand in his most of the time, no matter how often she pulled it away. But even the smoothest manners in the world could not make her trust him. Still, she couldn't seem to translate her distrust into disinterest, not physically anyway. Her skin would heat whenever he was close to her, and the smallest thing became highly provocative: the way he cupped her chin and directed her gaze when he wanted her to look in a certain direction, his knuckles brushing against her cheek, his fingertips skimming her hair, his hand settling in the small of her back as he escorted her. Every touch seemed to affect her in a myriad of ways, and the worst part of it was that he seemed to know it.

Often she would turn and find him staring at her, not that he tried to hide it. Quite the contrary, in fact. He seemed to enjoy watching her. Sometimes it seemed he did nothing else! It made her uncomfortable, especially as his attentions grew more pointed and pronounced. And yet, despite everything, she could not maintain even a reasonable distance from him. She employed a variety of tactics, beginning each encounter with a different mien. She pretended aloofness and eventually worked herself up to hostility, and yet, with Joel as accomplice, he invariably overcame her defenses.

It was no wonder that Joel was so taken with him and only natural, she supposed, that he should want her to see his uncle in a complimentary light. However, when Joel began to hint that Weston's attentions were amorous, she got worried. At first he only hinted, making not-so-subtle comments about how considerate Uncle Wes seemed to be, how much he liked her. Soon, however, he was teasing her about having a boyfriend! She had no recourse except to adamantly insist that he had misconstrued his uncle's behavior.

"He has to be nice to me," she told him. "Otherwise I might not let him see you."

Joel snorted at the notion of this. "Why wouldn't you want me to see Uncle Wes? That's silly. He knows you wouldn't do that."

But it wasn't silly at all; she just had no way to make him understand, innocent that he was. She tried another tack.

"Actually, Joel, Wes is not the sort of man I could be interested in. Really. I like a simpler sort of person, a predictable type." It sounded perfectly reasonable to her. She believed every word of it, but the sly slant of the boy's eyes said he didn't buy a single syllable.

He shook his head and brought his hands to his hips. "Momma always said you were backward about men. Guess she was right."

Joy was dumbstruck. *Momma always said you were backward about men.* Had Cynthia really said that? Obviously she had, and because she had, Joel obviously felt he was better equipped than she was to know what sort of man would make her happy. Moreover, he seemed to believe just what he wanted to about them. Of course he did! What could be easier for him than having the two people he loved most love each other? After all, if they were together, he wouldn't have to choose between them.

But how, without hurting him, could she make him understand that she didn't want to be a means to an end for Weston Caudell? Weston's interest in her was based solely upon the fact that she was guardian to his nephew. That was not enough for her. It would never be enough for her, but she had to find some way to convince both Joel and Wes.

That proved a difficult task over the next several days. Though Weston's attention greatly disturbed her, she ignored him, believing that eventually he would weary of the game and throw the full brunt of his charm against his nephew. It was the nephew who was the real problem now. He seemed to be waiting for her and Weston to fall headlong into love, to be convinced, in fact, that it was inevitable. She tried to reason with him, but he merely assumed this mantel of childish wisdom and smiled this sly, secretive smile, counseling her all the while to be confident and bold. It was maddening. And it became more so as time wore on.

Spring grew brighter and warmer, and Joel chafed at school and craved adventure, which he looked to Wes to provide. His uncle did not disappoint him. They went hunting with a camera instead of a gun, Wes explaining that while tracking and identification of the prey was the same, and one still possessed a trophy of his triumph, no blood was ever shed or life destroyed. Joy respected the viewpoint he espoused but resented being coerced to join them, a tactic that each employed with harrowing subtlety and skill. She felt more trapped than the animals they tracked, but she dared not protest too loudly.

They had fallen into a kind of arrangement. She maintained custody of Joel and Weston maintained generous visitation rights. As long as the balance was not upset, she suspected they could go on in this manner—no litigation, no threats, no tug-of-war with Joel's emotions. But were she to threaten to cut off access to Joel, were she even to *appear* to threaten to cut off access to Joel, she felt sure Weston would immediately pull out the stops and file for custody of his nephew.

All that stopped him now was the fact that he had no reason for contesting her guardianship. He couldn't complain about the way she took care of Joel, and he hadn't been able to dig up any dirt on her because there wasn't any dirt to dig up. So, lacking an excuse to declare himself an enemy, he played the part of suitor. It was the only plausible explanation. And she had no choice except to play along.

So it was that she found herself in the company of Weston Caudell on a regular, if not a daily, basis, and so it was that on a particular mid-May evening she came to sit on a hard stone bench in Weston Caudell's backyard, her chin on her hand, her elbow on the edge of a stone table, glumly watching as Wes and Joel turned steaks on the enormous new grill Wes had recently constructed. She was hungry, and her stomach made gurgling sounds as if to remind her of that fact, yet she couldn't seem to muster much enthusiasm about the meal. Life had become horribly complicated of late. She looked at Joel and Wes there with their heads together, laughing and joking, looking for all the world like father and son, and her spirits sagged lower and lower. She couldn't begrudge Joel this moment of happiness—or any other for that matter—God knew he'd had few enough in his lifetime—but she felt drained and threatened, as if life had become a perpetual walk on a tightrope, thanks, of course, to Weston Caudell.

For a moment Joy hated the man. Oh, why did he have to come to Folly Creek and reveal himself to Joel? But the next instant she felt ashamed. Weston obviously loved the boy. He had gone to incredible lengths to prove that fact. He had kept tabs on Joel for years, with Pritikin Marsh's help. He had moved to Folly Creek to be near him. He'd literally courted the boy, and he'd compromised with her when doing so. He had even gone so far as to pretend a romantic interest in her in order to assure himself of access to his nephew. Even though she despised his methods, she understood his motives only too well. Sighing, she folded her arms over the top of the stone picnic table and cradled her head upon them, exhausted physically as well as emotionally and mentally. It was not a good time for confrontation.

Joel walked up and laid an oven mitt in front of her, confrontation, no doubt, the last thing on his mind. "Uncle Wes says I should call and see if Sean can come over and eat with us," he announced happily. He leaned closer, speaking in a low, conspiratorial tone. "I think he wants to be alone with you. Why don't you go over and talk to him?"

He had been pressuring her of late to encourage Weston's suit, and no matter how foolish she declared the notion to be, she couldn't seem to get it into his head that it was a bad idea. She was even tired of trying. She lifted her head, looked him straight in the eye and said, "No."

"Aw, come on, Joy," he whispered urgently. "Don't be shy. Just go over and talk to him."

"I'm not being shy," she told him tersely. "I don't want to talk to him."

"Of course you do! Why wouldn't you?"

"Joel, he's your uncle, not mine."

"What's that got to do with anything?" he wanted to know.

Joy put a hand to her head, trying to think how to handle this, but she was just so tired of the emotional wringer, so frustrated by Joel's stubborn lack of comprehension that she couldn't handle it any longer. Her hand hit the table with a muted plop.

"Will you leave me alone about this!" she snapped. "I'm sick and tired of your harping!"

"Fine!" he shot back, wounded and confused. "Be that way! I was just trying to help—"

"You're not helping me!" she cried. "If you really want to know, you're being plain selfish!"

He looked as if she'd struck him. His jaw clamped shut, and his bottom lip protruded. For a moment she thought he was going to cry, but then he balled his hands into tight fists and backed away, shouting at her.

"If that's what you think, then fine! You don't have to put up with me. I've got real family, you know!"

Joy gasped, the arrow finding its mark smartly. In an instant she was on her feet, regret flooding through her, but it was too late for amends. Joel turned on his heel and ran to meet his uncle, who was already striding their way, having doubtlessly overheard at least the angry sounds of their voices. Joy watched in shock as the boy poured out his version of the confrontation, fists swiping angrily at bitter tears. After a few brief moments Weston sent Joel into the house. The boy trudged off obediently, while the man strode toward Joy.

"What on earth has gotten into you?" he demanded. "You've been as irritable as a grizzly on a winter morning."

"Well, thank you so much!" she retorted. "You, of course, being perfect, can't understand how that could happen."

"I didn't say that."

"You didn't have to."

"Could we just discuss this rationally, please?"

"Oh, so now I'm irrational, am I? Well, who wouldn't be, dealing with you all the time?"

He brought his hands to his waist, his brows butting together. "How the hell did this get to be my fault? I've bent over backward to please you! I've tied myself in knots over you, and now you're telling me that your moodiness is somehow my fault?"

"That's exactly what I'm telling you!" she shouted.

They glared at one another several seconds, then an amazing thing happened. He grimaced, and when his face relaxed again, the anger was gone. He sighed and shook his head, the semblance of a smile curving his lips.

"Why can't you just stop fighting me? Why can't you just let happen whatever's going to happen between us?"

"Oh, you'd like that, wouldn't you?" she said petulantly. "Well, I'm not going to let you manipulate my feelings. I'm not going to let you . . ." She found to her chagrin that she didn't quite know how to phrase it, but she plunged in anyway. "I'm not going to let you . . . stir up . . . needs in me."

He folded his arms and grinned maddeningly. "Do I stir up *needs* in you?"

She blinked at him, color flushing her cheeks. She hadn't said *that*, had she?

"You're obviously going to twist everything I say," she told him, trying valiantly to save face, "so let's just drop it!"

"I don't want to drop it," he said flatly.

She stared at him, casting about for some avenue of escape but finding none. Her frail hold on composure snapped.

"All that ever matters is what you want, isn't it?" she demanded. "It's beyond you to think of me or even Joel!"

"You know better than that," he began, but she wasn't up to any more.

She skinned both shins bolting from between the bench and the table, but the need for respite made her oblivious to mere physical pain. She didn't even realize for several moments that he was following, calling her name as she fled across the darkened, forested yard. Almost as soon as she recognized the sound ringing in her ear as her own name, he caught her, his hand closing around her arm just below the elbow. He stopped and yanked, bringing her hard around and against him.

It was more than she could bear. The will to fight had run out of her. She had already surrendered to her own misery, and tears were coming fast in low, muffled sobs. He grasped her with both hands and shook her so that her head fell back and the weak light caught the tears as they slid down her face. She didn't know what she expected, gloating, anger, disgust, but the very last thing on that list would have been tenderness.

"Oh, honey," he said, his voice as soft and warm as a down comforter. "Please don't." He lifted a hand and carefully wiped away the tears striping her cheeks. "It's all right. Everything's going to be all right."

He gathered her against him, holding her tight and stroking her hair while she cried against his shirt front, frustration upon frustration pouring out. He continued talking to her, whispering gently that he hadn't meant to wound, that he knew she was frightened, that all would be well if only she'd trust him, until she almost believed it, until she *wanted* to believe him.

And why wouldn't she? It felt so safe to be there in his arms, to grip the sides of his shirt and just hang on, letting him comfort her, letting all the pent-up emotion pour out, hearing that it was going to be fine. The war was over. No one had lost. Life was simple again. She wanted so much to believe that when he nuzzled her ear, whispering soft words whose tone registered more accurately than their meanings. She failed to summon her thoughts but snuggled against him, turning her cheek to the hard wall of his chest and trembling with a long, drawn-out sigh.

When he brought his hand around and gently nudged her chin up, she didn't even think of pulling away. And when the dark shadow of his head covered her face and his mouth drew near, she found it wholly natural, so much so that she turned her own mouth up to greet it, as if she had long been doing so from time immemorial.

His mouth closed with hers, and his arms tightened about her, and an ache deep within her seemed to subside to pleasure. She let him push her head back, her own arms sliding about his waist as his mouth held hers and parted it. His tongue slid inside, gently lashed about in the slinky softness, then grew turgid and curled against her own, inviting it to follow as he withdrew between the sharp even edges of her teeth. Then his tongue teased hers within his own mouth, encouraging her to explore, so that she tasted its soft sides and hard, arching roof, marveling in its warm sweetness.

The part of her that knew this was folly had retreated, while the part that craved this contact came slowly awake and stretched and reveled and asked for more. He seemed to sense this, deepening the kiss and running his hands over her back, shoulders and hips, pressing, kneading, fitting her against him, his mouth joined to hers, his tongue plunging and sweeping and inciting her own, until desire had not only weakened her but taken command.

For a long, heated, breathless time he held her, introducing her to the hard contours of his body and the pleasure of mating them to the rounded suppleness of her own. Her fingertips found their way into the tight pocket on his hip and the sleek fineness of his hair, and her mouth gave itself up to his, until at last, some need in her sated, she turned her face away and pulled the sweet night air into her lungs.

They stood with arms clasped about one another, and Joy laid her ear against his chest and listened to his heart until her ragged emotions were soothed and the beat became steady and slow. Presently he moved his hand to stroke her hair, then dropped a kiss on the crown of her head. As if in response, her empty stomach rumbled, and he chuckled softly.

"Come on," he said, stepping back and urging her forward with his arm in the small of her back. "I've got a steak over there with your name on it."

Suddenly, she felt timid and self-conscious. "Oh," she said. "Wait. Joel."

He adopted a conversational tone. "You never know what to expect out of kids, do you? But don't be too concerned. He'll come around and apologize before long. He knows he shouldn't talk to you like that. He's probably regretting it already. Don't think about it. Concentrate on yourself just now. Hey, I'd better get back to those steaks or we're going to be eating charcoal." She allowed him to lead her back to the table, talking in that chatty tone. "You work too hard. You know that, don't you? You need a good meal and a long rest. A steak, a full night's sleep and you'll be right as rain tomorrow. Uncover that salad, will you, hon?"

She uncovered the salad and he went off to fetch the steaks. It was strange how subdued she felt, as if her brain had gone on overload and just shut down. Wes brought a plate and set it before her. It contained a juicy steak and a baked potato wrapped in foil. He instructed her to eat and went into the house for Joel. Mechanically, she began to saw at her meat. She was sawing off her third bite when Wes and Joel came out together, arm in arm.

"We've decided to invite Sean over another time," Weston told her. "Tonight's for family."

Family. They were family in a strange, convoluted manner, he and Joel in one way, Joel and she in another. Joy said nothing but placed the chunk of steak she'd cut off into her mouth. It was perfect, just the way she liked it. Or was she so hungry she couldn't tell the difference?

Joel came over and sat down beside her. For a minute or two he was glumly silent, then his hand crept out and settled upon her arm. "I'm sorry," he mumbled. Then, louder, he said, "Honest, Joy, I didn't mean it." She put down her knife and fork and slipped her arms around him.

"Eat your dinner. We'll talk about it tomorrow."

A plate materialized in front of him, and Wes set a steak on it. Joel took up his utensils and went to work. "Good," he said around a hefty bite. Wes smiled and started piling salad onto his plate.

They ate in near silence. Joy felt content for the first time in weeks, her suspicions at bay, her physical needs met. She was Scarlet O'Hara, putting off until tomorrow the troubling thoughts of today, but she didn't care. She was too tired to care. They finished their meal and cleaned up. Wes backed the Suburban out of the garage. Joy and Joel got in front with him, Joel in the middle, and as they rode toward home, Joel laid his head on Joy's shoulder and closed his eyes.

She looked out the window at the black sky and felt the weight of his head, and the thought came to her that somehow it would be all right. Wes didn't really want to come between them. Maybe he *was* just trying to take the path that would guarantee him a place in Joel's life, and maybe he did see her as that path. But maybe, just maybe, if she gave him time, if she gave them both time...

But no. She put the thought away, retreating once more into the vacuum of exhaustion.

She woke in the pre-dawn, flushed with the sensations of his kiss, and thought, *He's winning. If I'm beginning to trust him, he's winning.* Or was he trustworthy, after all, and she only now was beginning to realize it? She didn't know what to think anymore.

She got up, bathed, dressed and went into the kitchen to find Joel sulking over a bowl of cold cereal. She asked him what was wrong, but he merely shrugged and said he didn't want to go to school. She laid her hand upon his forehead. It felt cool and smooth to the touch.

"You don't have a fever," she told him, "I don't suppose you have any symptoms you'd like to tell me about?"

He shook his head. "Wes is coming over. He called while you were in the bathroom."

She went to the counter and put the kettle on to boil. "What's that got to do with you not wanting to go to school?"

"Nothing," he muttered, getting up from the table. "And I've changed my mind. I sure don't want to hang around here all day."

She started to reply to that, but just then there came a knock on the door. Sighing, she walked through the living room and went to open the door. Joel followed, but the instant Wes was inside, he huffed off to his bedroom. She gave Weston a questioning look.

"I'm afraid I hurt his feelings," he said. "I let him know I wanted him to make himself scarce this morning so I could speak to you in private."

"Oh." That explained Joel's mood and gave her a pretty good idea of what he wanted to talk about. She steeled herself for another unpleasant encounter. The very last thing she wanted to do was hash over what had happened between the two of them the night before, at least not until she figured out exactly what that was. He asked if they could sit down, and she walked over to the sofa and took a seat. He sat down next to her and leaned forward, folding his hands.

"About last night," he began. She visibly stiffened, but he went on without pause. "I'm not sure how we should have handled that, but I do think we may have gotten off to a poor start. When you think of it, not many children have the complete attention of two adults, and maybe we—I—have been a bit too anxious to please."

She was having a hard time following. She'd expected the conversation to be concerned with what had happened between her and Weston. Nevertheless, she was only too glad to switch gears. "You mean Joel," she said with a good deal of relief.

He smiled. "Of course, I mean Joel. Who else? I didn't like the way he spoke to you last night, and it's not just for your sake. Children have to learn respect. That's one good thing my father taught me. See, I figure we have to present a united front. If he knows we both expect a certain standard of behavior from him, he won't be able to play us off against each other."

Now she really was taken aback. Since when had Joel's guidance and discipline become a shared responsibility? "You think we should present a united front," she repeated for clarification. "The two of us."

He looked at her like she'd sprouted daisies out of the top of her head. "What's with you? Didn't you get enough sleep last night? Who else is going to raise this kid if the two of us don't? Never mind. I don't even want to think about that. The point is, he shouldn't be able to get away with being disrespectful."

Well, this was surprising. She bit the inside of her cheek, wondering if he meant what she thought he did. There was, of course, only one way to find out. She licked her lips. "Is this your way of telling me that you're not going to take me to court over Joel?"

He studied his hands before leveling his gaze at her. "I don't see any point in that. It certainly wouldn't make Joel happy. It might even be counterproductive. I'm content with the current arrangement."

Again she felt relief, but only on an immediate level. She knew too well that he could change his mind at any time. She wasn't off that tightrope yet, but at least she had a better chance of keeping her balance. While she retained custody of Joel, she was still obligated to cooperate with Weston. He wasn't out of the act at all. He'd just decided to accept a co-starring role. She could live with that if she had to, but meanwhile she had to get something straight.

"Wes, Joel wasn't completely at fault last night," she confessed. "I blew up at him. I was tired and cranky, and something he said set me off. I know it sounds immature, but I've been under a good deal of stress lately and . . ."

She didn't want to give away too much, and she faltered, losing some of her bravado. Wes reached over and took her hand in his.

"I want to help," he said, as if he hadn't the least inkling that he was the source of her problem. "I want to help in every way I can. Joel needs both of us right now. It's important that we be in agreement as much as possible, and I think we need to try for a little more balance—for Joel's sake."

She wasn't quite sure what he was saying, but she had no intention of upsetting the balance just then. Time would tell how sincere he was, and until she knew that she wanted neither to alienate him nor become too deeply entangled. All she could do at the moment was nod and smile. That seemed to be enough. He squeezed her hand and got to his feet.

"Good. Good. Well, I'm glad we're agreed." He seemed prepared to go, and yet his hand still clutched hers. She wondered if there was something else on his mind, and he

PRESENTS

A Real Sweetheart of a Deal!

PEEL BACK THIS CARD AND SEE WHAT YOU CAN GET! THEN . . .

Complete the Hand Inside

It's easy! To play your cards right, just match this card with the cards inside.

Turn over for more details . . .

Incredible, isn't it? Deal yourself in right now and get 6 fabulous gifts ABSOLUTELY FREE.

1. 4 BRAND NEW SILHOUETTE ROMANCE™ NOVELS—FREE!
Sit back and enjoy the excitement, romance and thrills of four fantastic novels. You'll receive them as part of this winning streak!

2. A LOVELY GOLD-PLATED CHAIN—FREE! You'll love your elegant 20k gold electroplated chain! The necklace is finely crafted with 160 double-soldered links and it's electroplate finished in genuine 20k gold. And it's yours free as added thanks for giving our Reader Service a try!

3. AN EXCITING MYSTERY BONUS—FREE!
And still your luck holds! You'll also receive a special mystery bonus. You'll be thrilled with this surprise gift. It is useful as well as practical.

PLUS

THERE'S MORE. THE DECK IS STACKED IN YOUR FAVOR. HERE ARE THREE MORE WINNING POINTS. YOU'LL ALSO RECEIVE:

4. FREE HOME DELIVERY
Imagine how you'll enjoy having the chance to preview the romantic adventures of our Silhouette heroines in the convenience of your own home! Here's how it works. Every month we'll deliver 6 new Silhouette Romance™ novels right to your door. There's no obligation to buy, and if you decide to keep them, they'll be yours for only $2.25* each! And there's no charge for postage and handling — there are no hidden extras!

5. A MONTHLY NEWSLETTER—FREE!
It's our special *"Silhouette" Newsletter* your privileged look at upcoming books and profiles of our most popular authors.

6. MORE GIFTS FROM TIME TO TIME—FREE!
It's easy to see why you have the winning hand. In addition to all the other special deals available only to our home subscribers, when you join the Silhouette Reader Service™, you can look forward to additional free gifts throughout the year.

SO DEAL YOURSELF IN – YOU CAN'T HELP BUT WIN!

* In the future, prices and terms may change but you always have the opportunity to cancel your subscription. Sales taxes applicable in NY and Iowa.
©1990 HARLEQUIN ENTERPRISES LIMITED

You'll Fall In Love With This Sweetheart Deal From Silhouette!

SILHOUETTE READER SERVICE™

FREE OFFER CARD

4 FREE BOOKS • FREE GOLD-PLATED CHAIN • FREE MYSTERY BONUS • FREE HOME DELIVERY • INSIDER'S NEWSLETTER • MORE SURPRISE GIFTS

YES! Deal me in. Please send me four free Silhouette Romance™ novels, the gold-plated chain and my free mystery bonus as explained on the opposite page. If I'm not fully satisfied I can cancel at any time but if I choose to continue in the Reader Service I'll receive 6 Silhouette Romance™ novels each month for only $2.25 with no additional charge for postage and handling.*

215 CIS HAYR
(U-SIL-R-06/90)

First Name ____________ Last Name ____________
PLEASE PRINT

Address ____________ Apt. ____

City ________ State ________ Zip Code ________

Offer limited to one per household and not valid to current Silhouette Romance™ subscribers. Orders subject to approval.

SILHOUETTE® NO RISK GUARANTEE

- There is no obligation to buy - the free books and gifts remain yours to keep.
- You'll receive books before they're available in stores.
- You may end your subscription at any time—by sending us a note or a shipping statement marked "cancel" or by returning any shipment to us at our cost.

©1990 HARLEQUIN ENTERPRISES LIMITED

PRINTED IN U.S.A.

Remember! To win this hand, all you have to do is place your sticker inside and DETACH AND MAIL THE CARD BELOW. You'll get four free books, a free gold-plated chain and a mystery bonus.

BUT DON'T DELAY!
MAIL US YOUR LUCKY CARD TODAY!

If card is missing write to:
Silhouette Reader Service, 901 Fuhrmann Blvd., P.O. Box 1867, Buffalo, NY 14269-1867

NO POSTAGE
NECESSARY
IF MAILED
IN THE
UNITED STATES

BUSINESS REPLY CARD
First Class Permit No. 717 Buffalo, NY

Postage will be paid by addressee

SILHOUETTE READER SERVICE™
901 Fuhrmann Blvd.
P.O. Box 1867
Buffalo, N.Y.
14240-9952

didn't keep her guessing. "I meant what I said before about wanting to be your friend," he told her. "And now that we're joining forces, so to speak, I think that's more important than ever, so I was wondering if you'd join me one evening soon, for a movie perhaps?"

A date? He was asking her out on a date! But, of course, she couldn't go. On the other hand, did she dare refuse?

She blinked up at him and he stood there waiting for her answer. She felt the warmth of his hand and the sheer power of his presence, and she thought about how easy it had been to let him kiss her, not once but twice now. Just the memory of those moments made her breath draw short and her body awaken in ways that frightened and dismayed her. She knew she couldn't take the chance. The question was no longer whether or not she could trust him but whether or not she could trust herself. She stood and extracted her hand from his in the same fluid movement, as if one naturally involved the other.

"I—I really don't have much time, Wes," she managed. "Joel keeps me so busy and . . . I wouldn't be comfortable leaving him on his own." She tilted her head, still searching for excuses.

His response was an understanding nod. "Oh, sure. I should have realized. Just forget about it. Now, I'd better get out of here. I don't want to make you late." He dropped a kiss on the top of her head, his hands lightly skimming her shoulders, and turned for the door. "Tell Joel I'll see him later," he said, pulling the door open. He walked out and left the door standing, his footsteps sounding loud and hollow on the planks of the little porch.

Joy listened as he descended the steps and strolled down the cobbled walkway. She didn't know what she'd expected, but it wasn't what had happened. Mechanically, she stepped forward, and her fingers closed upon the smooth doorknob, but her mind was elsewhere. He had asked her for a date, and she had turned him down *after* allowing herself to be kissed and hearing that he wasn't going to take her to court—yet—and still he had accepted her refusal calmly and good-naturedly, like a true gentleman. Now if she only knew what that meant, this puzzle that was Weston Caudell might become clear.

What sort of man was this? she wondered. Cad or prince? Friend or foe? That was the sixty-four-thousand-dollar question, but she had too little data as yet even to make a guess. Oh, she had no doubt that he was both intelligent and confident. Neither could she question his determination, at least not where his nephew was concerned. And who could deny his charm? But plied toward what end, for what reason? She didn't know what to think, and she didn't dare let down her guard until she could be sure, until she knew what kind of man Weston Caudell really was—if that day ever came. One thing was for certain, though: he was full of surprises, just chock full. And then some.

Chapter Six

Despite her doubts, life took on a kind of normality for Joy. She got up every weekday morning and went to work. She came home again in the evening to Joel and, more often than not, to Weston. But Joel's budding relationship with his uncle was no longer the focus of the boy's life. The summer baseball league was beginning to form. Joel had failed to win a spot on the school team at the spring tryouts, and that failure had come at a time when his spirits were particularly low, and now he saw a chance to redeem himself. It wasn't enough merely to play, however, as everyone who showed up at tryouts would be assigned to a team. Joel's goal was to win a spot on the first string, perhaps even an infield position, and Weston had promised to help him do it.

Like so many adolescents, Joel seemed to have pinned his self-acceptance to this one area of performance. Past failure haunted him. Possible success taunted him. He was miserable. He was elated. He was desperately determined.

Joy, who was of two minds on the subject, could only support, encourage and caution, while Weston worked hard to help the boy improve his skill and self-confidence. This did not make for a stress-free environment.

Joel was uptight constantly, certain one minute that he could do it, certain the next that he'd humiliate himself. Joy worried that he'd be crushed if he did not attain the success he craved and would be dependent upon his uncle if he did. Only Weston seemed steady and on course, and about this, too, Joy harbored conflicting emotions. She didn't know whether to be grateful to the man or to blame him for the current problem. His promise to help Joel achieve his goal had raised the boy's hopes, encouraged him to reach farther than he ever had before, and she didn't know whether that was good or bad. She did not voice her fears, but she had to question whether or not Joel could bear another loss. Only time would tell.

Time. It disappeared in swings of the bat and the slap of leather. There were few moments to worry about Weston's ulterior motives or future betrayals; yet she did wonder. Every time she saw his face, she wondered. Even when it became commonplace to walk into her home and find Weston Caudell at ease there, she wondered what the future would hold for her and Joel. But life was just too busy to second-guess every decision and suggestion. The end of the school year was upon them. Tryouts were about to be held.

Joy and Weston went together to the last parents' meeting of the semester. It was both uneventful and awful. Everyone treated them as a couple. It was as if they had entered into a public partnership, the ramifications of which she could not guess, and it neither began nor ended there.

Weston provided easy transportation, and though there was no place in town that couldn't be reached by foot within half an hour and plenty of others who were quite willing to give a lift whenever needed, Joel just took it for granted that they were going to ride with Wes. Even Wes seemed to take it for granted. He stopped by unasked any time they had someplace to go, and it did make a certain kind of sense, as more often than not Wes was going there, too. Consequently, they began showing up all over town together—church, the library, the local pizza parlor, but most of all the ball field.

As the tryouts drew near, they spent more and more time there. Joy could easily have stayed home during these coaching sessions, but she didn't like the idea of just handing Joel over to Wes even for a short time. So more evenings than not she could be found sitting alone on the rough, splintery bleachers behind home plate, calling out encouragement while Wes handled the instruction. She had to admit that he was good at it, a fact that became obvious when Joel not only passed muster but was actively recruited by two different teams.

Joel was elated; Joy was both relieved and regretful. Weston had become the hero of the hour, and Joel told everyone who would listen. People were impressed. The league director asked Wes to consider coaching a team the following year. Everyone talked about what a difference he made with Joel. Joy felt the noose pulling tighter and tighter.

Weston Caudell was a man with a mission, and he seemed to have the patience of Job and the determination of Noah. He never made a decision involving Joel on his own. He continuously consulted with her and deferred to her judgment and authority in all matters pertaining to the boy. And he put himself at their constant beck and call. Even when Joel began to take him for granted, he remained cheerful and willing. Joel would say, "Wes'll do it." "Wes'll take me." "Wes won't mind," and Wes would come through, providing Joy said it was all right.

She should have felt at peace. Both Joel and Weston seemed satisfied with the status quo; yet she felt increasingly that change was inevitable, and however she looked at it, she seemed destined to come out the loser. She knew Joel loved her, but he adored his uncle, and suddenly she had nothing to offer him that Weston couldn't. Wes was a part of his life now, a big part. In fact, he'd made himself such an integral part of Joel's existence that he now had as much to do with the continuity of that existence as Joy did. He was real family making his presence felt in a real way. In addition he didn't seem to be limited by such mundane concerns as money, time and convenience. He was strong competition, everybody's fair-haired boy, and he made it all seem as effortless as yawning. Joy began to prepare herself to lose Joel, knowing that when she'd lost him, she'd have lost everything. She began to think about how she would rebuild her life when the worst came to pass.

Perhaps it was this budding pessimism that made her take a second look at Lee Jackson Goode. She had known the Goodes a long time. Mr. Goode Senior was a retired farmer who, along with his soft, gray-haired wife, made a habit of visiting Ball's soda fountain. Both were small and round, like animated garden gnomes in coveralls and zippered smocks. Mr. Goode almost always wore a striped engineer's cap set askew upon his balding head, while his wife carried a cloth bonnet tied to a narrow belt hidden between the plump rolls of her gingham-covered waist. They were pleasant people who often shared the same soda and held hands in public, their shy smiles offered in hopeful affability.

Lee Jackson seemed to have little in common with his parents. They were small and fair and elfin, while he was big and dark with a weariness in his face that seemed foreign to the elder Goodes. He looked out of place in the coveralls his mother starched and ironed for him and seemed an uncommonly private individual.

Joy, like everyone else in town, knew that he had once been married and that he and his wife had lived up north somewhere. It was said that he'd worked his way up the ladder in some factory, only to find himself laid off when the economy took a downswing. Rough times had apparently busted up an already shaky marriage, and there were a pair of little girls who no longer saw much of their daddy since he'd moved south again to work the farm his father was no longer strong enough to keep going. Some said he'd taken his losses really hard, and Joy felt a certain empathy for him, so when he came in one morning for a late cup of coffee, looking down in the dumps, she took a little extra time to chat.

"How are you keeping these days, Mr. Goode?" It was a standard question, asked almost as many times a day as she poured the coffee, but she put a bit of warmth into it just for him. He nodded, pulled his cup and saucer closer and took his first sip.

"You're Joy Morrow," he said, putting the cup down again. She smiled.

"That's right."

"My ma says you're raising some orphan boy."

"Trying to," she answered. "His mother had a hand in raising me."

"I remember her," he said, unusually talkative. "She sure did die young, God rest her."

"Yes she did." She couldn't help thinking that there was more than one way to lose a person, and his suddenly mournful expression prompted her to say as much. He nodded sagely, taking the comment exactly as it had been intended.

"Divorce is a kind of death, too," he said. "Kids grow up and move off. Friends drift away. Everybody loses somebody, I guess, one way or another."

It seemed that they were on the same wavelength, and the thought occurred to her that they also had a good deal in common. She lingered.

"You don't seem very interested in that coffee," she said. "Maybe you'd like something else?"

He shook his head. "Just to talk. Sometimes a man just needs to talk."

"All right."

She folded her arms over the countertop. He sipped again, killing time, and planted his elbows on the edge of the counter, hunching forward. "They say you go around with a fella named Caudell," he commented idly.

She pretended amusement. "Do they say he's thirteen?"

He grinned. "No, they don't say that. They say he's an uncle of your boy."

My boy, she thought, savoring the phrase almost gratefully. "Well, that would be Weston," she said, hoping no further explanation would be needed. "He's fond of Joel."

Lee Jackson Goode wrapped his big hands around the cup, overlapping them. "I don't know the fellow. Seems like all the folks I know around here are older. Just about everybody I went to school with has moved away or gotten lost somehow or other. Sometimes I think I haven't really come home at all."

Joy understood how he could feel that way. Without Joel, Folly Creek wouldn't be the same for her, either, now that Cynthia was gone. She didn't know what to say, so she said nothing at all. He drank his coffee and cooled his palms on his jeaned thighs. Suddenly, he pushed his cup away.

"People speak highly of you, Miss Morrow, and I'm thinking you might be a good person to know. I could use a friend, someone to talk to now and again. I guess I'm asking you out."

Well, well, she thought to herself, just when she thought her options were limited . . . But did she want to go out with Lee Jackson Goode?

"I don't know," she said. "I haven't been getting out on my own much. Kids just seem to take so much time."

"You'd best enjoy that while you can," he said, unknowingly hitting her where it hurt most. "Kids have a way of getting lost, too. If nothing else, they just grow up on you."

"So they do," she said with a little laugh. And so they did. She shrugged. "Maybe if I knew what you had in mind . . ."

He focused on her face. "There's a gospel singing over at Mount Horeb Church on Saturday night. I find that a pretty uplifting experience. Maybe we could try it."

Joy smiled. An uplifting experience was exactly what she needed. "I never knew anybody who had too many friends," she said. "I could sure use another."

He grinned and stuck out his hand. "Guess I'll see you Saturday."

She put her hand in his. It was big and hard and callused. "Guess so."

They shook on it. Afterward, he swiveled off the stool and fished the correct change out of his pocket, slapping it onto the counter. It did Joy good to see the smile on his face and know she'd put it there. Joel could manage without her for one Saturday evening. After all, he had Weston to keep him company. She wondered if he'd even miss her—if either of them would.

* * *

Joel was not pleased when she told him about Lee Jackson Goode. He had nothing against Lee Jackson, or so he said, but he'd planned on asking a couple of friends over for the night.

"Maybe you can still ask them," she said. "Maybe Wes will come over and supervise until I get back."

He admitted that was a likely option, but he still had his reservations. "Don't you figure you'll hurt Wes's feelings by going out with Lee Jackson Goode?" he wanted to know.

"Certainly not," she answered flatly. "Wes has no part in this."

"But he asked you out once and you didn't go."

She wondered where he'd gotten that bit of information, not that it mattered. "One thing has nothing to do with the other," she told him. "Besides, Wes and I don't have anything in common—except you, of course."

"And just what do you and Lee Jackson Goode have in common?" he demanded.

She folded her arms and began to pat her foot upon the floor, a sure sign that she was annoyed. "You wouldn't understand," she insisted. "And it really isn't any of your business."

He couldn't very well argue with that, but it didn't make him any happier about the situation. His freckled brow furrowed with dark thought. Joy sighed and pulled him close.

"Listen you, I have a right to my own friends, and that's just what Lee Jackson is, a friend, nothing more. Now stop thinking like a frustrated matchmaker, will you? And lighten up. It's not as though we're going to some den of iniquity. We're going to a gospel singing, for Pete's sake. What could be more innocent and friendly than that?"

He nodded and smiled, but she knew his heart wasn't in it, and for the first time she began to wonder if going out with Lee Jackson Goode was such a good idea after all. The next moment, however, she reasoned that she had to go through with it if for no other reason than to convince Joel that he was wasting his time hoping for a romantic involvement between her and Weston. She wavered back and forth between those two premises over the next few days, but by Saturday she'd convinced herself that no harm could come of going out with Lee Jackson and something might even be gained.

Weston amicably agreed to sponsor Joel and his friends on the evening in question, and it was arranged for him to pick up the boys about half an hour before Lee Jackson was expected and take them to dinner. Joy figured that would give her enough time to finish dressing, greet Lee Jackson, and be gone before Wes brought the boys back to the house.

Everything seemed to go just as planned. Wes arrived right on time and herded the boys out to the truck. Joy ran upstairs to get ready. She'd chosen her attire with care, hoping to strike just the right cord, nothing too provocative, nothing too stiff. Everything was all laid out and waiting for her. She slipped into the airy, brightly flowered dress she'd chosen, turned back the cuffs on the raglan sleeves and buttoned the closely fitted bodice that gave way to a soft, full, knee-length skirt. She put on her good white pumps and brushed her hair straight back, holding it in place with a narrow band of grosgrain ribbon tied with a dainty bow. She clipped gold button earrings to her lobes, dabbed on a bit of perfume and traded her everyday purse for a small bag made of white straw. Thus adorned, she went downstairs to spread her skirt over the couch, smooth her hair, and wait.

Not three minutes later, she heard the sound of a vehicle pulling to a stop in front of the house. Slowly, she stood and faced the door, shook out her skirt and put on a smile. A moment or two later, a light knock landed upon her door. She reached for the knob, turned it and pulled—to find Weston Caudell standing on her doorstep. She felt as if she'd just been doused with a bucket of cold water. Weston just smiled and stepped inside.

"Well, don't you look pretty," he said, and his eyes automatically made a circuit of the room. "The kids are waiting in the truck. They, um, decided they wanted to rent a movie, and I offered to bring the VCR over here and hook it up, but I did want to check it out with you first, make sure you have no objections."

It did appear that he was merely being his usual careful, unassuming self, but his timing could have been better. She really didn't want him there when Lee Jackson arrived for some reason. Nevertheless, she smiled.

"That's fine with me if you really want to go to all that trouble."

He nodded, and she assumed their business was concluded, but then he headed for the television, saying, "I'd better just take a look as long as I'm already here. Don't want any surprises after I've lugged that thing over here."

That, too, seemed reasonable. Yet she felt just a bit of irritation. But then how long could it take to look at the back of a television? Five minutes or more apparently, because five minutes later he was still jiggling wires and studying connections. In fact, he didn't finish looking at the thing until Lee Jackson had driven up, parked, walked to the house and was standing at the door, at which point Joy was obliged to introduce them.

The two men shook hands, gave each other the once over and turned placid faces to her. She made small talk for a few moments, then reminded Wes that he had four youngsters waiting in the truck. She noted that they had already been remarkably patient. Smiling and apologetic, he took his leave, slipping out past Lee Jackson, who looked a question at Joy. She offered him a seat, which he declined, then pretended to look for her handbag, finding it just as he was about to point out that it was laying on the couch within clear sight. She dug around inside for a moment, checking the contents and killing time, but the delay was for naught. When she finally stepped through the door, the Suburban was still sitting there, its engine idling. Wes tooted the horn. Everybody waved, and Lee Jackson took her arm, literally propelling her up the walk. Finally the vehicle pulled out onto the street and they were alone.

They got into his late-model sedan and started off. The silence was at first rather tense, but as they drove along, he began to hum and Joy began to relax. Apparently the need for conversation didn't crop up too often with Lee Jackson. He said nothing, and she followed suit, content to just ride along.

Mount Horeb Church was far up on the mountain, and by the time they got there the singing had already started and the surrounding forest was full of parked cars. Lee Jackson picked a place about two hundred yards down the steep mountain road and eased in between two trees. They got out and started to walk. It was then that he was moved to speak, first to tell her how pretty she looked and then to comment that he surely wasn't the only one to have noticed.

"That Caudell's got an eye for you," he said, "and I thought you ought to know, if you didn't already."

She slowly shook her head. "Weston and I are on friendly terms because we have to be—for Joel's sake. But Joel's the only thing we really have in common. Any interest you might have seen in Weston Caudell's eye had to do with that."

He seemed unconvinced, but he didn't say more on the subject; instead he chose another. "I hope you like this singing," he said. "Nothing stirs my soul more than gospel. Up north they don't get much of it." He talked of boyhood memories of singings that went on all night long and into the morning, and then they were close enough to hear the music and the time for conversation had passed.

It turned out to be a most enjoyable evening. Joy had been listening to gospel music all her life, but she'd never been to a real singing before. Group after group took the little stage at the front of the simple, narrow church, and music poured out in a live, vibrating stream. The audience, most of which was made up of the singers themselves, were apt to join in at any given moment, and hand-clapping and foot-stomping were equally spontaneous. It was, indeed, an uplifting experience, and when it came time to go, Joy, having promised to return at a certain hour, did so with great reluctance.

The walk back to the car and the ride home were filled with comments about the experience they had just shared, the kind of half-formed remarks only knowing friends could make or understand. Consequently the return trip seemed short and easy. Back in her front yard, they both grew tense again, the question of a good-night kiss looming between them. *Well, why not?* Joy thought, curiosity getting the better of her, and she turned up her face. Lee Jackson made short work of it, placing upon her mouth a light, graceful kiss of three or four seconds duration. Joy was pleased to find the experience undisturbing. It was so much easier to relax with one another when all that sexual awareness was absent. They both smiled and thanked one another for a pleasant evening.

"We'll do it again sometime," Lee Jackson promised, and so it ended, her first real date in many months.

She stood a moment as he drove away, savoring the ease and comfort of it. Why, she wondered, couldn't it be that way with Weston Caudell? How wonderful it would be for everyone if they could truly become friends.

But Weston Caudell was not Lee Jackson Goode. For reasons that had little to do with Joel, she just couldn't relax around Weston. She kept wondering what he thought of her, how she looked, with whom he compared her. Was he really attracted to her? Did he find her dull or foolish or dumb? It was disconcerting, to say the least, to remember his kisses and find herself flushed with heat.

No, it could never be friendship with Weston Caudell. She knew that now if she hadn't before, thanks to Lee Jackson, a good friend indeed.

Wes was sitting on the couch watching the television when she let herself into the house. He smiled at her, stretched and sat forward, rubbing his hands over his face as if roused from a nap. Joy looked around the room, expecting to find Joel and company but failing to do so.

"They're camped out in the back," Wes told her, reading her mind. "I didn't think you'd mind."

"Not at all," she told him lightly. "Thanks for standing in, but I don't want to keep you."

"Oh, I'm all right," he said, stretching his legs out before him and making no move to rise. "How was the music?"

She stiffened automatically, then forced herself to relax. Putting her back to the door, she leaned against it, then crossed her legs at the ankles, her hands behind her. "Wonderful. I would have liked to stay longer, but I'm not much of a night owl." She yawned for emphasis, covering her mouth with a small fist.

"You're tired," Weston said in an understanding tone. "Come and sit down."

It was not what she'd had in mind. She began to wonder if she was going to have to ask him to leave. Pushing away from the door, she walked over to the sofa and sat down as far away from him as she could get without being too obvious. She spread her skirt out around her and lifted one hand to the back of her head. For a moment she concentrated on the television. A famous personality was conducting a shallow interview of a little old woman who had recently been elected sheriff of some small town in Texas. It was a rerun of a previous showing.

"I've seen this," she said. "It's not worth staying up for." He turned his head and smiled at her, seemingly missing the hint entirely. She found herself at a loss for words, yet felt she had to say something or sit watching television until dawn. She began carefully. "Weston, I really appreciate you being here for Joel. It's good to know I—*he* can count on you for, um, evenings like this."

"Well," he said, "glad to help. You don't seem to get too many evenings out."

She hadn't expected *that* reaction, and for some reason she didn't like it. Piqued and unsettled in a way she couldn't even explain, she folded her arms. Suddenly, he stood up.

"Well, I'm tired. I really ought to run along and get some sleep."

Relieved, she bounced up and followed him toward the door, only to have him stop dead and turn around, nearly bowling her over.

"Oops." He caught her in both arms and steadied her. Her heart clutched and stalled. For a long moment it seemed that it didn't beat at all. She thought, *He's going to kiss me,* and her mouth turned up of its own accord, no debate, no decision, just a natural reaction to being in his arms. She waited, resigned to her fate, and . . . waited.

"My mistake," he said, and stepped back. "I thought I ought to say good-night to the boys, but they're probably asleep by now and I'll see them in the morning anyway. I think I'll go on. Good night."

She just looked at him, frustration twisting inside her like a knife. If he noticed, he gave no indication. He merely smiled, turned around and walked away. It took her a moment to realize what was happening, then she snapped to and hurriedly followed him to the door, getting there just in time to have it close in her face. She was stunned, stunned and . . . disappointed.

She closed her eyes and laid her head against the door, confused, frustrated, appalled. He hadn't wanted to kiss her. Hadn't he wanted to kiss her? She had felt certain *before* that he had wanted to kiss her, even when there had been no opportunity to do so. Then, the opportunity had presented itself, and he'd turned around and gone home! Had she been misreading him all this time? What about those first two kisses? The man wasn't very . . . *consistent*.

Or was he? You could say he was consistently surprising, at least, but that didn't help her determine what was on his mind. What was he thinking? Was he glad to see her stepping out with Lee Jackson Goode? Maybe he thought she'd fall in love, get married, have babies of her own and forget all about Joel. Maybe he was hoping for that very thing. She felt betrayed somehow, wounded, and the realization that she was being irrational, not to mention foolish, did nothing whatsoever to blunt the force of the emotions she was feeling.

Play with her, would he? Well, she wasn't the hillbilly he seemed to think she was. All right, so she wasn't big city sophisticated. She made no apologies for that. She was small town, and she meant to stay that way, wouldn't, in fact, be anything else. But that did not give him license to come here and play fast and loose with her emotions. She hadn't even begun to match wits with the man, and it was time she showed him just what gutsy stuff she was made of. Maybe it was even time to turn the tables on him, play by his rules. Maybe she could teach him what it felt like to be toyed with—and maybe she could even get Weston Caudell out of her system in the process, think about someone else for a change, dream about someone else. Maybe then Lee Jackson Goode would stir more in her than sisterly concern and gratitude. Maybe then life could become normal and sedate again. Maybe, just maybe, she could even keep from breaking her heart.

Chapter Seven

Sunday morning was a new beginning. The tables were turning on Weston Caudell, and Joy was the impetus that made them spin. She was going to overwhelm the man with kindness and deference, if for no other reason than to keep him guessing. Her smile became a tool, her thoughtfulness a strategy, acquiescence a measure of control, and she wielded them ruthlessly.

She hauled out the sleep-over crowd early, feted them with a hearty breakfast, and begged, bullied, and bribed them into getting dressed. By the time Wes showed up, the tents and sleeping bags had been put away and the whole crew was decked out in their Sunday best and ready to go. He was pleasantly surprised, and Joy was sweet as sugar, thanking him again for taking over the night before, praising the camp-out idea and telling Joel how lucky he was to have such an uncle.

After services, two of the boys went home with their parents who were regulars of Preacher Marsh's congregation.

The third boy they dropped off on their own way home. Immediately afterward, Joy asked Weston to have Sunday dinner with her and Joel. He agreed instantly, and they made an afternoon of it. She put herself completely at his disposal, adopting his every suggestion with delight, and in the days that followed, she kept it up.

Whenever Joel would say, "May I?" she would purr, "Ask Uncle Wes." And when Wes would ask, "What do you think?" she would smile and shrug and blink her eyes and come back with, "Whatever you think." He would then make a decision, and she would instantly agree. It was all so incredibly easy that she wondered how she could have fallen for it these past weeks, but if Wes recognized his own modus operandi, he didn't let on. In fact, he took the mantel of authority without the slightest hint of reluctance, as if he didn't even know he was doing it. What's more, he was good at it, surprisingly good.

Joel, too, adjusted to the new system as if unaware anything was different. Joy wasn't thrilled about that. She was even a little hurt. It was as if she and Weston were interchangeable as far as Joel was concerned, but in truth his life changed very little. He still did the same things with the same people. He practiced and played ball three times a week. He hung out with his friends, rode his bike around town, fished, hiked, went to an occasional movie, attended church on Sundays, took too long in the shower, ate his dinners with Joy, Weston, or both. Weston had been around long enough to learn the ropes, and his decisions didn't vary much from those Joy would have made herself, so it was understandable that this change should make so few actual waves. Even her own life was outwardly the same, and yet, it wasn't. In fact, the only visible change didn't have a thing to do with Wes or Joel. Instead, it had to do with Lee Jackson Goode.

It was all very innocent, of course. She had found a friend, and as friends they were apt to get together and chat. The easiest place to do that was the soda fountain, and Lee Jackson quickly developed the habit of stopping by for a morning cup and a few minutes of idle chatter. Then one day the conversation took a decidedly serious turn.

It was a Monday, little more than two weeks after what was likely to be their one and only real date, for they had rapidly gotten beyond the possibility of romance and settled into genuine friendship. It was out of apparent concern for that friendship that Lee Jackson spoke, and it was natural that he should do so over the rim of a coffee cup.

"I had a visitor the other day." He paused to sip and gave her time for reply. Joy was polishing parfait glasses, but she glanced up to give him an encouraging smile.

"That's nice. Anybody I know?"

"Yep." He put down the cup and leaned forward in that earnest way of his, a sure signal that something was up.

She stopped what she was doing and gave him her full attention.

He cocked his head to one side, giving the words full impact. "Weston Caudell."

Joy's eyebrows went up in tandem. "Oh?" She adopted a disinterested tone, but it was an insincere effort meant to underline her concern.

Lee Jackson didn't mistake her meaning. He nodded and ran a fingertip across the countertop. "Surprised me a little. I mean, we're not exactly buddies, though he was nice enough. In fact, it's probably the nicest warning I've ever got."

"Warning?" she repeated. "I don't get it. A warning about what?"

Lee Jackson grinned crookedly. "You."

She was thunderstruck. "Me! *Me?*" Lee Jackson nodded affirmatively.

"What he said was that I ought to 'pursue other interests,' but what he meant was that I ought to keep my hands off."

"Hands off," she echoed, the meaning of this starting to dawn. "Are you saying he warned you to stay away from *me*?"

"That was the general idea, yeah."

She smacked the countertop with her fist, then immediately threw up her hands. "Of all the nerve! Who does he think he is?" She fell back against the mixing counter and shook her head. "I can't believe this! He's got no right to go around warning off my friends!"

Lee Jackson wiped a hand across his mouth. "Well, the way I see it, he either thinks he has the right or he wants it."

That gave her pause. She chewed the inside of her cheek reflectively. After a moment she shook her head again. "This doesn't make sense. What did he hope to accomplish?"

Lee Jackson chuckled. "Well, that's pretty obvious. He meant to clear the field for himself."

That would explain an otherwise inexplicable situation, and despite a certain amount of anger, she felt a surge of exhilaration. Was it possible? Could he truly be interested in her apart from Joel? *Romantically* interested in her? But she couldn't dwell on this, not now.

"What did you say to him?"

Lee shrugged. "I said I didn't want any trouble with anyone, but that you and I are friends and I expect it to stay that way."

"What did he say then?"

"He said something about everyone needing friends, shook my hand, asked if we understood one another, got in his car and left."

"And you're sure you didn't misunderstand?"

He grinned. "Oh, we understood one another all right. No doubt about that."

She took a deep breath, the implications of this beginning to dissolve her initial anger, and his grin widened.

"I thought you'd want to know."

She didn't know what to say to that, so she just said, "Thanks."

"You bet."

"It won't happen again," she promised. "I'll see to it."

"No problem," he assured her. "Hey, what are friends for?"

She smiled and refilled his cup. What, indeed?

He either thinks he has the right or he wants it. Lee Jackson's words kept running through her head all day long. *He either thinks he has the right or he wants it. He meant to clear the field for himself. We understood one another all right. He either thinks he has the right or...* Did he really want it? Had he intended for her to know? And what on earth was she going to do about it?

It was funny how a bit of new information could transform a whole outlook. The more she thought about it, the more it made sense, how sweet and cooperative he'd been, the way he'd made himself a place in their lives, hers as well as Joel's, the kisses, the little touches, the long looks and ready smiles. She'd been making something sinister out of this, when all along he'd been rather obvious, not pushy, but obvious—and so very patient.

And now what? It seemed that the next step was hers, but in what direction ought she to go? What happened next could very well change all the rules for both of them, not to mention Joel.

Joel. Had he really been right all along? Had he somehow known Weston's intentions and desires? She wanted to believe he had. She wanted to think it had been more than wishful thinking, but then again, what divine fulfillment it would be if Weston really had come to care. Joel would be so happy and so smug, as if he'd made it all happen, and maybe in a way he had, but she wasn't quite ready to let him in on this. Not yet. She had to know first. She had to be sure. It was the only way, and it promised to be plenty tricky, but sooner or later she was going to get her chance.

In the meantime she carried on as usual, except that her life wasn't the same, of course. Cooperation was no longer a game, but became instead the natural order. It was amazing how quickly they adapted once deference became genuine, how easy it was to divide the responsibility and the decisions. She had her job and the responsibility of making a home for Joel. Wes had his work, which turned out to be surprisingly complicated, and coordinated transportation and entertainment. Discipline became a combined effort. On this score, they were finally presenting that united front of which Weston had spoken weeks, now months, ago. And yet, they seemed to be walking on eggshells with one another, not that it was immediately obvious to anyone but the two of them.

Wes remained bright and calm and easygoing. There were moments when he seemed to be reaching out to her, when casual things seemed loaded with import, things like reaching over to tuck her hair behind her ear or squeezing her hand or sitting next to her when other seats were readily available. Sometimes it was nothing more than a look or a word spoken softly in agreement, a tone of voice. Still, she held back, waiting, watching. Finally the moment came.

It was a weekday evening. Weston had thoughtfully brought take-out barbecue for their dinner, and a game of Scrabble had been planned for afterward. Joy had dressed with care, as had become her habit of late, trading her work clothes for a pair of slender capri pants of cool blue cotton and a matching top cropped at the waist. Sensible shoes had given way to sandals, and she had brushed her long hair until it lay smooth and gleaming upon her shoulders, refreshed her cologne and darkened her pale lashes with mascara.

Weston was already in the kitchen taking waxed cartons out of a paper bag when she came down. He turned and smiled when she entered the room. "His lordship is washing up, and without a word from me, I swear. Seems like our boy's growing up more and more every day."

"Seems like," she agreed, relishing that possessive pronoun. "Thanks for bringing in dinner. It's nice to get out of kitchen duty every once in a while."

"Just don't forget to leave a tip," he quipped. "Now what'll it be, chopped beef or sausage links?"

"Both," she decided. He gave her a wink.

"A woman after my own heart."

Was that a twinkle in his eye? she wondered, feeling warm and hopeful. Joel came in, and the atmosphere subtly altered. By silent agreement they sat down to table and said grace, Joel doing the honors himself.

Wes played host and dished out the goodies, piling their plates with tasty meats and all the fixings: red beans, coleslaw and potato salad, dill pickles, crunchy radishes and carrot sticks, with thick slabs of grilled toast. It was tasty fare, but they all agreed the best part was not having to do dishes. Joel suggested they get a microwave and eat off paper plates from then on, but Joy and Weston quickly shot down that idea.

"I've formed a proper addiction to real home cooking," Weston admitted.

"And I like to set a proper table most of the time," Joy put in. "There's something about a proper table that's, well, proper."

They laughed at her, but they knew what she meant. Still, it was nice to skip the heavy cleanup for a change. She went to get the card table out for their game while the guys took care of the leftovers, an exercise that consisted of finding space in the refrigerator. They carted kitchen chairs into the living room to set around the card table Joy had brought out from the closet, and just when they'd gotten everything in place, the phone rang. Joel ran to answer, most of their calls being for him anyway, and for some minutes carried on a loud, lively conversation before covering the mouthpiece with his hand and turning to give them an excited, plaintive look.

"Please, can I spend the night at Sean's house? All the guys are going over there tonight so they can get up early tomorrow and fish. *Please?* Chuck says he caught a three-pounder up at Suttler's Branch with a dumb old grasshopper!" He went back to the phone, babbling excited questions about rods and lines and exact locations, while Wes and Joy exchanged questioning looks.

"It's been a while," Wes pointed out quietly, "and he's pretty excited, but there will be other fishing trips and if you think for some reason that he ought not to go, then—"

"Why not?" Joy interrupted brightly. "You're only young once. Besides, he knows how to handle himself around water, and that creek they're talking about isn't very deep anyway. I think it'll be all right."

Wes covered her hand with his and caught Joel's eye with a toss of his head. "Get off the phone and get your gear," he said, "and be careful riding your bike over to Sean's."

Joel whooped and put down the receiver, disappearing into the hallway.

"Well, there goes the game," Joy commented lightly, "unless you still want to play."

She got one of those direct looks that made her pulse start to race.

"Don't have anything better to do," he said. "Ladies first, but that's the only break you get, and I warn you—I am unbeatable at this game. I've memorized the entire unabridged dictionary."

"Ho ho," she quipped, "and I'm Charlie Chan."

"Why, Charlie," he teased, "what a fetching disguise. I especially like the hair, not to mention the eyes and that little shirt you're wearing."

Her heart was beating like the entire timpani section of a high school band, but she managed to laugh and say something funny in a bad Chinese accent. Joel breezed through with a hug for each of them, promising to be home by ten the next morning and to cut the grass soon afterward. Despite the distraction, she was able to play the word *sprint*, to which Weston added the letters *E* and *R*, grinning wickedly.

"How original. I do the real work and you collect the points."

He grinned. "It's a rare form of brilliance. Your turn."

She came up with *dynamo*, playing off his *D*, and hooted when he spelled out *nil* off her *N*. "How appropriate."

"Scoffest thou not," he intoned drolly. "The game is far from overeth."

"Overeth? On what page of the unabridged dictionary did you find that one?"

"Let's see. I believe it was page 617."

"Maybe you should have memorized an *English* dictionary."

"Maybe I should have drawn your tiles instead of mine."

"Poor darling," she cooed, "all those smarts and no luck."

"Ah," he said, wiggling an eyebrow, "but I do so like the sympathy of a beautiful woman."

"Well, you're not getting any here," she sniffed, "however you flatter me."

"Simple truth is not flattery." He looked her squarely in the eye. "And the simple truth is that you are a beautiful woman."

A warm glow radiated through her, pinking her cheeks and putting a demure smile on her lips. She looked down at the lettered tiles on her tray, seeing at once what she was going to do next.

"It seems I'm a few letters short," she lied, and reached for the bag of undrawn tiles, dumping them on the tabletop next to the board.

"Now why didn't I think of that?" he cracked, watching while she quickly searched out the needed tiles. "What an excellent strategy, cheating."

She arranged the tiles, spelling out K-I-S-S-M-E, and turned the board to face him. He stared at the strange collection of letters, while Joy's heart sat in her throat. Then he carefully pushed the board away from him.

"Lady," he said, his smoky gaze coming up to meet her clear blue one, "I like the way you play this game."

He got up from his chair and came to get her, lifting her gently to her feet. He stroked her hair away from her cheeks and took her face in his hands, turning it up at a slight angle. "I've waited so long for this," he told her softly, and bent to brush his lips across hers. "So many times I've wanted to take you in my arms." And then he did.

She lifted her hands to his shirt front, feeling beneath her fingertips the soft fabric of a simple striped sport shirt and the hard, solid, muscled flesh beneath. His heart was telegraphing a rapid-fire tattoo, as was her own, and she smiled tremulously, in awe of what seemed positive proof that his desire equaled hers. He cocked his head slightly, his gray eyes finding hers and holding them, drawing her closer and closer until she could feel the warmth of his skin on her nose and cheek. Her eyelids floated down, and her whole body seemed to bask in his nearness. His mouth settled against hers, and her lips trembled, beckoning, and finally welcoming as his arms tightened and his mouth ground down, taking full possession.

She opened to him, lips and teeth parting, and his moist, sweet breath mingled with hers. His tongue slid into her mouth, and she lifted her arms about his neck, moaning softly, mindlessly as her breasts met the wall of his chest and his embrace tightened yet again, pressing her length against him so that her soft curves flattened and filled the tautly molded planes of his body. His tongue delved deeply. His hands lightly massaged her back, stroking and pressing again and again. She felt the slight, almost unwilling, thrust of his hips, the hard masculine ridge of his need of her, and the spasmodic response within her own body, the tightenings and the openings and the gathering of moisture as if her femaleness hungered for his male sustenance. She wanted him to make her whole in a way she had not imagined nor, therefore, understood. Her senses railed at the impossibility of it. Some part of him seemed to recognize the silent turmoil and to take heed.

He lifted her against him as easily as if she were a doll. Her body slowly rose as his mouth took hers again and again. As her mouth rose out of reach, he moved instead to the soft underside of her chin. His teeth captured the tender flesh, his breath heating it, his tongue stroking it, and then moved downward. He tasted the column of her throat, causing her breath to catch. Her head fell back as bolts of electricity shot through her. Her hands gripped his shoulders; her fingers convulsed with each jolt. His mouth forged a searing path to the swelling of her breasts beneath the thin cotton of her shirt, breathing fire through the soft fabric to harden the nubby peaks against the feathery nylon of her bra. She felt as if she were about to burst, as if she couldn't contain the building crescendo of sensation, the throbbing clamor of desire.

Then she felt herself lowered again, her body creating a delightful friction against his, their clothing pulling, straining, snagging. She raised her hands into his hair, and his mouth immediately came to claim hers. Her fingers laced together at the back of his head, increasing the pressure of the kiss. But the moment her feet touched the floor, his mouth parted from hers, his hands left her sides, and he swept her up, stooping quickly and smoothly to bring his arm beneath her knees. Straightening again, he cradled her weight against him. She had no idea where he was taking her, but it hardly mattered as long as he touched her, held her.

She laid her head against his shoulder and slid her fingers through his hair, feeling herself transported. They left the brightness of the parlor for the shadowy hallway and turned to the right. He shouldered open a door that stood partly ajar and moved stiffly upon painted hinges. She saw the pale walls and the pink filmy curtains, the little wardrobe in the corner. They were in the front bedroom, Cynthia's room. Joy felt the smiling, loving presence of her dearest friend.

He bent and laid her upon the bed, Cynthia's bed, with the worn chenille spread she had smoothed with her own hands and the crisp sheets upon which she had never slept and yet were somehow hers, too. Joy felt again as she had felt so long ago, as if she'd found haven and home and need no longer fear being lost and alone. He eased himself down beside her, down onto Parker's bed, his brother's bed, where happiness had been made, where love had been bred. Cynthia and Parker, they were part of it, and yet none of it as he took her in his arms.

She looked up into his handsome face, followed the outline of it with her eyes, and knew she loved him, wanted him, needed him as Cynthia must have loved Parker, pined for him, hurt for him. She understood suddenly why no other man could ever have taken his place and felt closer to her friend for having understood at last.

She lifted a hand to brush back a wisp of hair that had fallen over his forehead, and again that smile of awe curved her lips. He dropped a kiss into the hollow of her throat, and his hand lifted her shirt, his fingers gathering the fabric as it rose against her skin. He brought his head up and took her mouth again, the hot breath from his nostrils fanning her cheek. With his hands he pushed up her shirt, his fingers sliding over bare skin, making her gasp into his mouth when they found the thinly sheathed mound of her breast. She felt the rise and fall of her chest beneath the welcome weight of his hand, and the air in her lungs became heady, intoxicating, so that every breath brought her closer and closer to a dizzying, mindless, exquisite need.

He was no longer merely taking her mouth, but allowing his to be taken in turn. She wanted him closer. She slipped her arms about his neck, arching against him, and his hand left her breast, sliding downward over midriff and waist and hip before sliding beneath her. She turned onto her side and let him press her against him, molding her body to his, and still it was not close enough to sate this craving. He thrust his knee between her legs, and she responded naturally, rhythmically, knowing her role in this rite with the genetic instinct of all womankind. Time-honored, magical, this act would bind them together as nothing else could, meld their bodies, their hearts, their souls. Here. Now. Upon this dear old bed of Cynthia's and Parker's, this marriage bed, this *marriage* bed . . .

Suddenly she thought of Cynthia and Parker and how it must have been for them. She thought of the sacrifices they had made to be together, of the rejection they had suffered to be joined by love and law and holy decree. They had no right to be there upon that bed, she and Weston. As badly as she wanted this, she mustn't do it, for then there would be no going back.

And could she and Weston bear what Cynthia and Parker had borne? Could she ask him to give up what Parker had given up? To live as Parker had, for his wife's sake alone?

And what of Joel? Must he bear a second rejection, a repeated loss? She couldn't do this. She wouldn't.

She rolled away onto her feet beside the bed, staring down at him. His arms were thrust out, as if he couldn't quite believe they didn't hold her.

"We can't do this!" she gasped. Wes blinked at her, as if he failed to understand. She lifted a hand to her mouth, appalled with both of them, herself for letting this happen, him for not understanding why it couldn't.

He grimaced and sat up on the bed, one knee drawn up, one hand pushing through his hair.

"Is it this room?" he asked softly, looking about him. "It's her room, isn't it? Cynthia's." He pressed his hand against the bedspread. "Cynthia's and Parker's." His voice held a wealth of emotion, but Joy knew it had as much to do with the brother he missed as with her.

"Don't you see?" she said. "If we repeat their mistake, we'll have the same result."

"That's absurd!" he said. "They loved each other. They made no mistake!"

"They couldn't know how hard it would be," she argued. "Cynthia didn't understand how much Parker would have to give up!"

"This isn't about Cynthia and Parker," he said sternly. "This is about you and me."

"And Joel," she added. That seemed to give him pause. He sighed and put his head back against the wall, the top rail of the old iron bedstead supporting his back.

"You're quite right," he said. "We do have a responsibility to Joel."

"And to each other," she said.

He sighed again, the sound heavy with resignation. "And to each other." He rubbed his hands over his face, then turned to the side, swinging his feet off the bed. He got up slowly, reluctantly, and bringing his hands to his waist, turned to face her across the bed. "I meant to be patient. God knows, I've *tried* to be patient. But you must know how long I've wanted to do this."

She wrung her hands, her thoughts tumbling together in confusion. "I—I think I do, but it still seems so *impossible*. I mean, you're just not like me. You have everything—money, choices, family. I only have Joel. I—I know you love him. I know you'd do anything to be with him, but you don't have to..."

He stared at her. "Is that what you think this is about? You think I want to sleep with you to assure myself access to Joel?"

"I... No! I mean, I only know that I'm not ready to..." She cast about for the proper words. "T-to commit myself to...something that may not be right for everyone. We're not the only ones involved here. There are others."

His hand went to his face and then to his hips again. "Like who? Uh, besides Joel."

"Like your parents," she said, "Joel's grandparents. Like them."

He lifted his shoulders. "What about them?"

She couldn't believe he didn't get it. "Weston! Look what they did to Cynthia and Parker! Look what happened to them!"

"You aren't suggesting my parents somehow caused the deaths of my brother and his wife?"

"No! I meant the rejection, cutting them out of their lives. It must have been heartbreaking. It must have hurt so. You know Parker was hurt, and because he was hurt, Cynthia was hurt, and because of them, Joel."

"And you think it's going to happen all over again if—*when* my parents find out about us."

"Isn't it?"

He looked at her, and a slow smile came to his face. "Come here," he said, but even as he said it, he started around the end of the bed. She met him halfway, and he pulled her into his arms again, holding her close, tucking her head beneath his chin. "What am I going to do with you?" he whispered into her hair. "You're serious about this, aren't you?"

She nodded. "Yes, I think I am. It didn't occur to me before. All I could think of was losing Joel."

"Well, that's understandable," he said, "considering the way I mishandled the thing in the beginning."

"It would've taken time," she admitted bluntly, "no matter how it was handled."

He rocked her gently in his arms. "I—I understand that," he said haltingly, "but I need to know: did it... Does it have anything to do with Lee Jackson Goode?"

She smiled against his shirt front. "You went to see him, didn't you?"

He blew out a breath. "You know about that, do you?"

"Lee's my friend," she said. "Friends tell each other what they need to know."

"You're not mad at me then?"

She tilted her head back, smiling up at him with his answer in her eyes, and there was his mouth, so close, so tempting. She went up on tiptoe and brought her lips to his. Her arms tightened about him, and she splayed her fingers across his back. He increased the pressure on her mouth accordingly, his hands beginning to roam over her body. She wanted him so. Why should she think of the Caudells or the pain they could cause when euphoria was so near? But no. Love meant so much more than momentary ecstasy, so much more. She forced herself to withdraw.

"You have to go," she said sternly. "I don't trust myself to be alone with you."

He laughed and tried to pull her back. "Trust *me* then."

"Ha! Out. Go on. Now." She pushed his hands away, turned him, aimed him toward the door. He went reluctantly, dragging his feet down the hallway, across the living room.

"Spoilsport."

"Seducer."

"Oh," he said, opening the door, "you're going to regret that."

"Promise?" She pushed him out onto the porch. He kissed her again just to show that he meant it, pulling her out onto the little porch with him and doing a most thorough job of it. When she pushed away this time, she was smiling softly and trembling.

"If I could only make you understand," he told her without banter, "how much this new life I've found means to me. I understand Parker so well now, and I think I needed to understand. I guess that's part of why I came here to find his son."

She touched his cheek lightly with her fingertips. "I know."

"Do you?" he asked softly.

She nodded. "I went looking for love once," she told him, "and I found Cynthia and Joel."

"And I found Joel and you," he stated simply, but she bit the inside of her cheek and shook her head.

"It's not the same. I had nothing and no one to lose."

"And I do?"

"You have your parents."

"And they aren't apt to accept you any more than they were Cynthia, is that it?"

"A big part of it, yes. Joel, after all, is their grandson, but I'm no part of them. We're as different as day and night, and even if we were both sure, I don't think I could stand between you and them. I know what it's like to live without the love and care of parents."

"So do I, in a way."

"You only think you do."

He seemed unable to refute the logic of that. He stood in the porch light a long while, thinking, weighing. At last he squinted into the darkness.

"You've given me a lot to think about," he admitted slowly, and then he grinned. "And since I'm not going to get much sleep tonight . . ."

"Oh, go take a cold shower," she scolded good-naturedly, and he laughed, then nodded.

"Good night," he said.

"Good night."

He went slowly down the steps, then strode off into the darkness. Joy turned away, unable to watch him go, and hurried inside. She closed the door and turned the lock, then switched off the overhead light and stood in the darkness, listening as the truck started up and the tires began to crunch the gravel at the edge of the road.

Only then did she let herself feel it. Only then did she dare let it out.

"It can't be," she said. "You know it can't be."

Chapter Eight

It seemed to Joy that the only thing to do was to retreat. She couldn't give up Joel, and she couldn't ask Wes to give him up. There just seemed to be no other option except to keep her distance, as impossible as that sounded, and try to work around those errant feelings and desires. It didn't take Wes long to get the message. The fact that she nearly ran every time he came near her made her position fairly clear, even though they never really discussed it. She was afraid to talk about the situation, afraid she'd be talked into something that would ultimately be bad for all of them.

It was not Weston's way to push, she knew, and she counted on that. He didn't disappoint her, but denial could be a two-edged sword. Mostly she was glad that he didn't press her, but there were times when his seeming indifference hurt like torn flesh, when she wanted him to throw his arms around her and declare, "Enough!" But then what would be the good in that? His acquiescence seemed to say that he agreed with her, that their feelings could not survive the rejection of his family, the destruction of his life as he knew it. Lee Jackson told her flatly that she was a fool, but when she asked him how heavily the acceptance of his own parents weighed with him, he couldn't answer her because he couldn't imagine being without them.

Only Joel seemed unaffected by the silent turmoil surrounding him. Life had acquired a new focus recently, the baseball challenge having been met. He wanted a tree house—and not just any tree house but the castle of tree houses.

Wes seemed glad to oblige, saying the physical labor involved would be good for him. It took him a couple of weeks to arrange his schedule so that he had the time to devote to the project, but one day Joy came home to sounds of hammer blows and saw strokes.

Joel and Wes had chosen a large oak out back at the edge of the woods. A tall boulder had been thrown down against it at some point beyond memory, and because of the boulder lying at its base, it had grown at an odd angle, thrusting its lowest, strongest limbs out to one side, the bottom one a mere four feet from the ground. As a result the tree formed a kind of stepladder on that one side to a middle level, where the branches grew more normally, shading not only those below but the boulder as well. It was on that middle level that they anchored Joel's tree house to two strong branches.

Joel was ecstatic from the moment work began, and Wes seemed to take a certain grim enjoyment from the activity himself. He had bought a truckload of new equipment for the construction—saws, hammers, levels, squares, a whole keg of nails and enough lumber to build a mansion—which was pretty much what they did. Ten feet square with a real door and shuttered windows on every side, shelves and a lock box and a terrace, it was the Windsor Palace of tree houses.

Palaces, of course, are not built in a day. They worked for more than a week. Stripped to the waist, bodies glistening with perspiration, rolled bandanas tied about their damp heads, their hands encased in dirty gloves, they hauled and cut and hoisted and hammered, until at last the final nail had been driven, sealant had been painted over every square inch and water-tight caulking had been forced into every crevice. She got the grand tour, not once but repeatedly, then was banished so the gang could properly christen the place for sacred male doings. Joel was the envy of his peers, and he magnanimously declared the place "club" property. Joy was so happy for him and proud. The frightened boy, too small for his size and bearing his wounds in moody silence, had grown into a strong young man with the gleam of confidence in his eyes and a heart as big and open as the sky. She blessed the day Weston Caudell had come into his life—and dreaded the day he would leave hers, for increasingly she came to believe that was how it must end.

And less than a week after the completion of the tree house, the beginning of the end seemed to have come.

It was a Thursday, and all three of the Goodes had stopped by for malteds. She was surprised to see them, for it was not their custom to come into town in the afternoon, but she was always glad to have them around, especially Lee. She'd already made two of the icy confections and was working on the third when the telephone rang.

The store had only one telephone, an ancient rotary dial model with a frayed cord encased in black electrical tape. As it was located in the sundries portion of the shop, Mr. Ball usually answered it himself. But as sometimes happened, he had stepped out for a moment, leaving Joy to dash the full length of the store in order to take the call.

"Blast!" she muttered, quickly turning off the blender. "Wouldn't you know it?"

Lee Jackson chuckled. He turned on his stool, planted his elbows on the bar top and openly watched as she dashed down the center aisle, her smock tail flying. The elder Goodes busily slurped their strawberry malts, huddled together like teenagers. Joy vaulted the low, swinging gate that separated the sundries department from the sofa fountain and grabbed for the phone.

"Ball's Sundries and Soda Fountain."

"Hello, Ball's Sundries and Soda Fountain. This is Weston Caudell."

"W-Wes?" She knew she sounded breathless, and color diffused her face. "I had to run to grab the phone," she explained. "Mr. Ball has gone out."

"Oh." He sounded apprehensive. "Does that mean you won't be able to get away for a bit this afternoon? I need to talk to you."

It was an unusual request, but something about his voice told her this was important. She made an effort to remain upbeat.

"What is it, Wes? You sound serious."

"Do I?" He chuckled, and the sound made her feel a little better. "It's really no big deal," he told her, "but I'd prefer to talk about it in person, uh, and in private, if you know what I mean."

"You mean that you don't want Joel to overhear."

"Something like that."

Well, that explained why he'd called the shop in the middle of the day rather than simply speaking to her at dinner, but it raised a great many other questions as well.

"You're being very mysterious," she said.

"Am I?" He sounded surprised. "I don't mean to. But, listen, could we talk about this person to person. Do you think you could get away for a few minutes this afternoon?"

She took a deep breath. "I think so. Do you want to come here?"

He had an instant answer. "No. Why don't you come over here."

"To your house?"

"That's right. I'll stop by and pick you up if you like."

She shook her head, then realized what she was doing. "That's not necessary. I'll just walk over. How's four o'clock?"

"The sooner the better," he said, "but don't worry. I'll wait until I can talk to you."

Wait until I can talk to you? That seemed an odd way to put it, but there was no point in discussing anything now. "I'll be over as soon as I can," she told him, and hung up.

Joy walked slowly back to the soda fountain, wondering what was up. What didn't he want Joel to know? It all sounded positively ominous.

She smiled apologetically at Lee Jackson, not really remembering him at all, and began to wipe up the counter.

Lee Jackson Goode chuckled raspily. "Hey, what about my malt?"

Joy stopped scrubbing and blinked at him. "Oh, my gosh! I'm sorry! I forgot." She rushed to the blender and took the metal cup down. The concoction had clumped and was melting. Well, what had she expected? It was the middle of summer, after all. Quickly she dumped the watery chocolate down the sink and began to make another. In two minutes it was ready. She sprinkled some chopped almonds on top for good measure and included a spoon in the tall, frosty glass. Lee Jackson took it with obvious relish.

"Nothing important was it?" he asked, and spooned up a mouthful of chocolate and almonds.

Joy gave him a closed look. "I don't know. Maybe."

He nodded and waved his spoon around in circles. "Don't want to talk about it, huh?" She shot a look at his parents, who were paying close attention, and gave her head an almost imperceptible shake. "Must have been Weston," he commented, then abruptly changed the subject. "Listen, we're going for a ride later, the folks and I. We're going up over the mountain to the university. Want to come along?"

She smiled apologetically, her interest piqued. "I can't. What are you going up there for?"

He licked his lips and grinned. Mr. and Mrs. Goode nodded encouragingly. "I'm going back to college," he announced, "going to finish my degree."

"What special news!" She went up on tiptoe and threw her arms around his neck, giving him a quick hug. "How wonderful! Well, what are you going to do? After graduation, I mean."

He shrugged and sucked on his straw. "Teach school, maybe."

"Oh, Lee! I'm so happy for you, and look at you, you're beaming."

"It feels right," he said. "You oughta go back, too. It's an awful lot of driving in every kind of weather, but we could share rides maybe."

She laughed. "I'd like to go back sometime, just not now."

"Won't he be a fine teacher?" Mrs. Goode said proudly. "Farming's not for him. We told him to do what made him happiest, and this is it."

Joy couldn't have been more thrilled by the news, and she understood now that this was a special celebration. Her mood suddenly lifted, her own troubles momentarily forgotten, and she joined in the joy of the moment.

By the time Mr. Ball returned, the Goodes had finished their malteds and spilled out all the happy details of Lee's decision and were on their way out the door. She gave them enough time to make it to the corner before she let her mind go back to Weston and that disturbing phone call. Sighing, she untied her apron and approached Mr. Ball.

He was, as usual, gracious. "Well, I suppose turnabout's fair play," he said. "I can hold down the fort on my own for a while." She gave him a kiss on the cheek as she went out, wishing she had as much reason as Lee Jackson to be happy and optimistic.

It was hotter outside than she had realized, but she spared the temperature little thought as she strode swiftly along the sidewalk, turning in the direction opposite to her regular one. Within a quarter of an hour she was walking across Weston's shady lawn. He answered her knock at once, smiling.

"How about a cool drink? I bet you could use one."

"Yes, thanks."

She followed him through the living room and dining room, into the spacious kitchen with its modern appliances and gleaming countertops. He poured her a glass of lemonade from a tall iced pitcher and then poured one for himself. They sat at the breakfast bar on tall stools, and it was only after she'd slaked her thirst and was placing the glass on its woven coaster that she saw the leather bags sitting beside the door that opened to the garage.

"You're leaving!" She stared openmouthed as he pushed a hand through his hair.

"It's not permanent," he assured her quickly. "I'll be back when I can, but just now I've got to go. It's the only way, believe me."

"Why?" she demanded sharply, knowing she should have expected this, but he shook his head.

"Let's just say it's business, personal business."

It wasn't any kind of answer, but somehow that didn't matter any longer. He was going, as she'd known on some level that eventually he must. "And I suppose you want me to break it to Joel," she said.

He took a deep breath. "Yes."

Suddenly she wanted to hurt him, to make him feel what she was feeling at that moment. "So you're tired of playing uncle," she accused, "and it's up to *me* to tell him."

"It's not that at all," he told her, and this time the gentleness of his tone caught her, seemed, in fact, to envelope her. He took her hand in his, and all the fight went out of her. "Now listen to me," he urged. "I know what I'm doing. Trust me. Can't you do that?"

"You're leaving," she said, not knowing what else to say.

He turned her hand over in his. "We can't go on like this, Joy. We're both so unhappy."

"Joel's happy."

"But for how long? Eventually he's going to see beyond the facade, and then he'll be as miserable as we are."

"Maybe," she conceded, "but he'll be hurt *now* if you go without seeing him."

"Believe me, it's better this way."

"It can't be."

"It is," he insisted patiently, "because he'll ask questions it's best not to answer. Not yet anyway."

"Is it so much easier not to answer *my* questions?" she demanded angrily.

The stool screeched as he got up and pushed it away.

"Not in the least," he said, bringing her to her feet, "but you're an adult. Besides, I had to see you."

"Why?" she asked petulantly.

"Because," he said, taking her face in his hands, "I need this."

She looked up into that smoky gaze, so sincere, so amazingly tender, and she knew he was going to kiss her. She put her forehead to his and closed her eyes in exquisite pain from longing. He ran his thumb lightly over her mouth, then gently settled his own over it, his hands dropping away, his arms wrapping around her. She pressed against him, her own arms sliding about his waist, her mouth parting beneath his. He tasted of lemons, all sweet and tart at the same time.

He loosened his hold, his hands spreading in the center of her back, then sliding down to her hips. Surely and deliberately, he fit her body to his, his message personal and clear. He wanted her; that hadn't changed.

She took his tongue into her mouth and leaned into him, sending a message of her own. After a long while, he released her. His hands came up once more to hold her face, and he pulled his mouth from hers, his forehead moving into its old position.

"That's what I needed to know," he told her softly, and the lids slowly lifted over his eyes as he straightened. He smiled at her.

She wanted to poke him for thinking he could read her so easily, but his grin was infectious, so she just laid her head upon his shoulder, feeling its strength. "You will be back, won't you?"

He stroked her hair. "As soon as possible."

She sighed. "You really shouldn't, you know. Things haven't changed."

"Maybe I can change them."

"And if you can't?"

"I don't know. All I know is that I can't go on like this."

"And you can't give up Joel."

"Any more than you can."

They just held each other, taking comfort and renewing strength for the difficult time ahead. It was a long, lovely time before they separated again, and then only with difficulty.

It was much harder to let him go than she'd thought it would be, and she couldn't help wondering what it might be like the next time.

He kept her hand in his as they walked across the floor to the bags waiting beside the door. Together they loaded them into the truck, one large, one small, then he helped her into the front seat through the door on the driver's side. She slid no farther than the center of the seat, and when he got in next to her, he first started the motor, then put his arm around her, drawing her close. He backed the vehicle out of the garage and headed it down the street toward town.

Three minutes later he pulled to an easy stop in front of Ball's Sundries and Soda Fountain, put the transmission into park and got out. She slid beneath the wheel and out onto the ground. He caught her arm and held her.

"I'll see you soon, both of you."

She nodded and gave him a wan smile. "Take care."

"You, too. And tell Joel, well, tell him I'll miss him."

She promised she would do that, and he brought her back to him for one more lingering kiss. Then he got into the truck and drovc away.

She watched until he turned a corner and disappeared, then she went inside. It was here that she had first laid eyes on Weston Caudell. She hadn't dreamed then that when he left, he would take her heart with him.

Breaking the news to Joel was every bit as difficult as she'd expected.

"Well, how come he didn't tell me himself?" Joel wanted to know. "He never said anything about having to go off.

Besides, he can take care of all his business from right here. He told me so. He explained the whole setup to me."

Joy could only shrug. "All I know is what he told me, but I'm sure it was something important."

"That doesn't explain why he didn't tell me himself," he insisted glumly, and she had to agree.

"No, it doesn't, but he must have had his reasons. I'm sure it's for the best."

The boy nodded, but he wasn't any more pleased by this than she was.

She slipped her arms about his shoulders. Had he gotten taller of late? Yes, of course he had. Funny how that kind of thing slipped up on you. She gave him a squeeze. "Hey, it won't be so bad," she said halfheartedly. "We were doing pretty well before he came along, weren't we? We can survive a few days without him, can't we?"

He tried to perk up enough to smile, but they both knew Weston Caudell had become a big part of their lives. He settled for a nod and changed the subject. "What's for dinner? I'm starved."

Joy forced a smile and hugged him, feeling lost and vulnerable and uncertain. They were old and familiar feelings, dangerously reminiscent of childhood, and she realized suddenly that Joel was feeling the same way. But each of them had learned to live without people they loved. If they could survive the loss of parents and friends, they could survive this, given enough time. They *could* get along without Weston.

Meanwhile, they were *not* going to spend every day until Weston returned being miserable and sad. This was their time.

They went out to dinner that evening, and the next evening they went to a movie. They bused over the mountain to play miniature golf at a new course near the university, and after that Joy arranged for Joel and a few buddies to go horseback riding with a neighbor. She organized sleep-overs and fishing trips and television parties. They borrowed a grill and a picnic table and cooked out in their own backyard. They painted Joel's room four different colors and dyed his curtains and bedspread to match. It was fun and it was tiring and, coupled with the adolescent adventures that came so naturally to thirteen-year-olds, it made for a very busy ten days. And still she found time to miss Weston.

Joel did, too, if his moodiness was any indication. With a bit of effort she usually managed to coax a smile out of him, and after that he would perk up somewhat. They didn't talk about Weston. She made an effort to avoid even the mention of his name, and yet it was there, this unspoken word between them. In the dark of night, lying alone in her little attic room, she knew in her heart that it always would be.

Avoiding his name became a pattern. Her days were busy enough to hold all but momentary thoughts of Weston at bay, and yet her mind never seemed truly clear of him, especially at night. Not even sleep protected her from thoughts of him. Against her will, unbidden, memories came to her, memories of being touched and held and kissed, memories of a man's body and a man's desire and the soft whisper of his voice. In addition, as if memories were not painful enough, her mind conjured up fantasies for her. She dreamed of making love with Weston, of sleeping in his arms and waking to cook breakfast in her bathrobe while both Joel and he waited at the table, their hair uncombed, clothing hastily thrown on. She dreamed of his homecoming, of hearing the Suburban pull up in front and dashing out to meet him. He ran toward her, scooped her into his arms, kissed her. He was so happy to be there, and she was so happy to have him. Dreams. Just dreams.

Somehow, she'd lost everyone she'd ever loved—perhaps she even expected to—Joel included, though she wasn't prepared to face that yet. Not just yet. But soon? She didn't want to know. She couldn't make herself contemplate what the future might hold, and yet, deep inside her heart of hearts, she knew. She knew. And on the eleventh day Wes called to prove her right.

Joy wasn't even there to speak to him. She left the shop that evening and stopped at Edmond's Grocery to pick up some strawberries to go with the shortcake she intended to bake. She wasn't delayed very long, just long enough, it seemed, for when she came through the door, Joel was just replacing the telephone receiver upon its cradle. The face he turned to her was ashen and taut, and she knew at once that he'd just spoken with Weston.

"What is it? What's wrong?" She hurried to leave the grocery bag on the kitchen table and returned to him. "Was that Weston on the phone?"

He nodded, his face grave. "He said to tell you he'd see you soon."

She held her breath. "Was that all?"

He shook his head solemnly. "He wants me to meet my grandparents."

So it was true. She lifted a trembling hand to her forehead. Her mind began to race. He was trying to mend fences, to convince his parents to accept Joel. Of course he was. Joel was, after all, their grandson. Weston would want to secure Joel's inheritance if at all possible, not to mention his own, and he would want their blessing. It was natural to want the blessing of one's parents. She had no doubt that he also hoped to convince them to accept her as Joel's guardian. He wouldn't do anything else. She believed that. She chose to believe that. But surely he saw that it was hopeless. Or was it?

She took a deep, calm breath. "Are the Caudells coming here?" she asked. Joel nodded.

"As soon as they can arrange it, he said. Don't know when that might be." He shrugged and lifted both hands, palms up. "A few days maybe. Wes couldn't say."

Then at least the possibility existed. He wouldn't be bringing them here if it didn't. He wouldn't put Joel through this if he didn't believe it would work out. The least she could do was prepare things at this end.

"Joel," she began, "you do want to meet your grandparents, don't you?"

That shoulder lifted and dropped again. "I told him I would if he wants me to."

"And you know that he wants what's best for you?"

"Sure. I guess so."

She placed her hands upon his shoulders and shook him gently to make him look at her. "You don't have to guess," she told him. "You know that you can trust Wes, don't you?"

He sucked in his cheek, then dropped his head. "Yes."

Her brow furrowed. What else was there? Why the bowed head, the guilty look?

"Did he say anything else?" she asked. "Something that upset you?" To her horror, the boy's chin began to quiver.

"He said he loved me. He said that I was brave and good and that he was proud of me." Tears rolled down his face. He reached up and briskly wiped them away, eyes averted.

For one difficult moment she could do nothing but choke back her own tears. She put her arms around him and at length trusted herself to speak.

"It's all right to be frightened," she said. "But you must know that we won't let them hurt you. I promise."

He shook his head, looking at his toes intently. "It's not that."

"Then why the tears?" she probed gently. "Because you miss Wes?"

He stood very still, and she knew he was trying to get a grip on himself. "I—I didn't think he was coming back," he confessed, his voice breaking.

"Oh, Joel." She held him away from her and ruffled his hair, smiling reassuringly. "We all have doubts. That's normal. But you're the most important person in your uncle's life. You don't have to doubt that."

"I—I know." He scrubbed his eyes with his fist. "He went to so much trouble to get to know me. I just thought, you know, m-maybe something bad would happen, maybe he couldn't come back."

She held on to him while he'd let her. "I do know how that feels," she said. "You keep telling yourself it's all right, but then you can't help remembering when it wasn't."

"Yeah. I knew you'd understand." He sniffed and gave her a quick hug, the tears apparently conquered. "You always understand. That's what's so great about you."

"You're pretty great yourself," she told him, relinquishing the hug. "And Wes knows that as well as I do. It really is going to be okay, Joel. You just have to remember that change is sometimes for the better."

"Sure." He was feeling awkward now, scuffing his toe on the floor. Then suddenly he jerked his head up and looked her square in the eye. "You know, it's kind of like really having parents," he said. "I mean, I don't remember my dad, so it was just always Mom and I. Then you came, and it was sort of like having a sister, but now with Weston, well, it's almost like having a mom and a dad again."

A mom and a dad. She and Weston as a mom and a dad. The very idea made her insides turn to Jell-O. It was too much to ask for, too much to hope for. She couldn't let herself think of that. She couldn't let Joel think of it. The Caudells would never let that happen.

"I'm not old enough to be your mom," she told him briskly, "and even if I were, Weston's not your father."

Joel put his hands into his pockets and made a squeaking sound by twisting the sole of his shoe against the floor. "I know that. I just meant—"

"Never mind," she interrupted smoothly. "The important thing is that one of us, either Weston or myself, will always be here for you. You can count on that."

"I do," he said, but she knew that he hadn't disconnected her and Weston in his mind. How could he when she hadn't managed it herself? Yet.

"We'd better start thinking about dinner," she said firmly, derailing any further conversation. "I bought strawberries. How's that for a treat?"

"Oh, great!" he declared, and went immediately to the kitchen to wash the berries. Joy followed, forcing herself to go through the familiar motions with a stony smile, but she knew that nothing, no force of will, no depth of concentration, no chore, no food, no thought, could lighten a heart as heavy as hers.

Chapter Nine

Joy and Joel were out in the back when Wes came. Joel had pinned a hand-drawn target up on the graceful old black walnut tree down by the creek and was shooting arrows at it with a cheap bow loaned to him by a friend. Joy was watching and sunning herself, having dragged a lightweight folding chaise out into a patch of sunshine. She wore a halter top and a pair of cutoffs, her feet bare, hair swept up into a ponytail at the crown of her head. It was not exactly the way she'd have preferred to be found by Weston Caudell, but suddenly he was there, casting a long shadow across the ground. Every nerve ending in her body recognized the shape of those broad shoulders and lean torso.

She sprang up and twisted about to face him. He stood there and looked at her, his hands at his hips, the sides of his suit coat spread to reveal a crisp white shirt. She knew she looked a sight, but a slow smile spread across his mouth, and she noted with satisfaction that his gaze contained nothing of censure. He lifted a finger to his mouth and indicated with a nod that she was not to alert Joel. She turned her head to glimpse him just as he let the arrow fly, and next saw the shaft protruding from a black ring very near the center.

"Bravo!" Weston applauded the shot. "Well done."

Joel dropped the bow and ran to throw his arms about his uncle, to thump him on the back and stand off again, grinning.

"Welcome back!"

"It is good to be home."

He reached out and locked his arm around the boy's neck in what looked like a wrestling hold but was actually a manly hug. Joel wrapped both arms about Weston's waist and attempted to lift him but managed merely to disturb his balance. They tussled a moment, laughing, and Joy couldn't help thinking how alike they were. They could have been father and son, just as Joel had imagined.

She again became aware of Weston's eyes and lifted hers to meet them. They seemed almost blue today, with a secretive, intimate glow that made her think of their goodbye. She smiled at him, and he reached out for her hand. She delivered it into his larger one, her other going self-consciously to her hair, tendrils of which had slipped free of the rubber band.

He sighed and pinched the bridge of his nose. "I must apologize because we don't have much time. My parents will be here any moment. I want you both to run in and change. You—" he flipped a finger under Joel's nose "—face and teeth, please. And you—" to her surprise he planted a quick kiss on her mouth "—let your hair down for me. Oh, and cover those gorgeous legs. A proper lady never shows gorgeous legs except from beneath a skirt." His tone was flippant and his smile quick, but she could feel his tension.

"Run along," he said to Joel. Grinning ear to ear, the boy took off, arms and legs pumping.

Wes turned instantly to Joy. "You haven't said anything."

"I haven't had a chance."

"I don't want you to be nervous about this."

"It's just that I didn't realize they would want to see me, too."

"Why, my dear, you are the main attraction," he told her.

She recoiled with surprise at that ominous statement, and it was then that the smooth sound of an automobile engine reached them. She looked around to see a long black limousine climbing the hill.

"Blast!" Weston said. "Run on up. I'll let them in. And don't worry!" He gave her another quick kiss, this one landing slightly off-target, and ushered her toward the house.

It was all very disturbing—the Caudells coming here after all this time, Wes behaving so anxiously. And what was this business about her being the "main attraction"? She didn't like the sound of that at all, and neither, apparently, did Wes.

Pondering this, she hurried up to the relative safety of the attic, but even there she felt no real sanctuary.

She heard car doors closing as she shucked her shorts and halter, and dashed madly about the room in search of a bra. Finding one, she slipped the straps over her shoulders and sprinted to the closet, deciding on the spur of the moment to wear a trim white eyelet dress with a long zipper up the back and a flattering narrow, lined skirt. She ripped it from the hanger, opened the zipper, and stepped into the dress, yanking it up and over her hips. She plunged her arms into the short sleeves, frantically fumbled with the fastener on her bra for a moment, got it hooked, and began the struggle with the zipper. In one fluid movement she raised the zipper, yanked the rubber band from her hair and started for the mirror.

Grabbing the hairbrush, she slashed savagely at her hair, plumped it and tucked one side behind an ear, securing it with a little yellow bow tied to a clip. The brush hit the floor. She reached for a compact and lightly powdered her face, then found a tube of lip gloss, pulled off the cover and ran the pale pink color over her lips. Turning, she rushed back to the closet and scuffed around inside until she got her feet into shoes. Unfortunately they weren't mates, so she kicked one off and replaced it with a low, white pump, rather worn and too often polished but serviceable. She took a moment to draw a deep breath and compose herself, wishing she had time for stockings, then went down.

When she entered the living room from the kitchen, it was to find a tall, gray, dignified gentleman coming to his feet beside a slender woman who kept her seat upon the warm sofa. It was the woman who captured her attention. Her shoulders were held erect, her spine straight as a rod, and her rather blunt legs were crossed at the ankle and tucked back neatly. Mrs. Caudell was dressed in two-tone blue with simple gold-chain accessories and a paisley scarf pinned at her neck. Her salt-and-pepper hair was swept up into a taut roll against the back of her head, the front arranged in dramatic waves flowing from a center part, below which dark brows arched gently above deeply set, pale blue eyes. Her nose was straight and narrow, her mouth prim and sedately tilted at the corners, skin and teeth perfect. All in all, she was the epitome of old, proud money, but despite the stiff posture, there was something soft about her, something *motherly*, which for some reason Joy had not expected.

Mr. Caudell nodded mutely, standing at attention like a field marshal who had forgotten he was out of uniform.

Weston moved to her side at once and took her arm as if she were infirm or elderly. His quickness and solicitation revealed a deepening concern, and one look at the stern face of Calvin Caudell explained why. It must have been a daunting experience to stand before such a father as a child.

Weston made the introductions. "Mother, Father, this is, of course, Miss Joy Morrow. Joy, I'd like you to meet my parents, Ginjevine and Calvin Caudell."

"My pleasure," she said, smiling hopefully.

Ginjevine Caudell curved her mouth into a polite smile and nodded regally. Her husband merely sniffed, his eyes staring straight ahead. Quite subdued, Joy took a seat on a chair that had been carried in from the kitchen. Weston stood behind her, his hands upon her shoulders protectively. She wondered which of them he was protecting.

Calvin Caudell abruptly sat down and arranged his clothing to minimize wrinkles, tugging here and there at the dark tweedy fabric of his suit. This done, he carefully crossed his legs and looked up. As if on cue, Ginjevine Caudell began what Joy could only think of later as an interview.

"Miss Morrow," she said in her cultured voice, "I apologize if we caught you unawares. Weston gave us to understand that we were expected.

Joy smoothed her skirt, painfully aware of her bare legs. "We were expecting you," she explained. "We just didn't know when."

"If you recall, Mother," Weston put in tautly, "*you* didn't know when you would be able to make the trip yourself."

Ginjevine Caudell put a hand to her hair, smoothing the perfect roll at the back of her head. "Yes, it is true. Our schedules are terribly crowded. We usually plan weeks in advance. Sometimes months." She let her hand fall to her lap and smiled thinly. "I'm sure you know how it is. There are so many social obligations. You do understand?"

"Perfectly." Joy smiled. It seemed the gracious thing to do.

Calvin Caudell raised a pale fist to his mouth and coughed softly. Ginjevine's mouth thinned.

"We were wondering," Ginjevine began on cue, "if we might know your parents?"

Joy steeled herself. "No, I'm afraid not."

"I should have told you, Mother," Weston quickly put in. "Joy's parents died many years ago."

"An accident," she added, and his hands tightened encouragingly upon her shoulders.

Ginjevine flicked a glance at her husband. "How sad."

"Yes." Mr. Caudell paused to clear his throat, then went on abruptly. "How is it that you came to have custody of our grandson, Miss Morrow? I'm afraid I find that terribly confusing."

"Well," Joy explained carefully, "I came to live with Cynthia and Joel when I was seventeen. We were very close, the three of us, and since there really was no one else..." The Caudells stiffened, and she immediately broke off.

Mr. Caudell uncrossed his legs. "I see. So you were out on your own in the world at seventeen. Interesting."

Joy was about to reply to that when Joel walked into the room from the hallway. He was stuffing his shirttail into the waistband of a pair of corduroy jeans. His hair was wet but smoothly combed, and he was wearing his dress shoes with a pair of white socks. Joy remembered regretfully that she had left his dark socks pegged to the line strung across the mudroom. Wes left her to sling an arm about the boy's shoulders.

"Well, if it isn't himself," he declared cheerily. "Right this way, young sir. Your grandparents have come to meet you." He ushered the boy forward and made the formal introductions. "Joel, this is your grandfather." The two shook hands, Calvin Caudell looking painfully uncomfortable. "And this," Weston said, addressing the boy to Mrs. Caudell, "is your grandmother."

For the first time, Ginjevine Caudell seemed to melt. Her pale eyes sparkled with recognition, and she took both the boy's hands in her own, a shocked little smile forming upon her lips. "My, how like your father! Calvin, isn't he just like Parker?"

Calvin Caudell cleared his throat and looked mortified. Ginjevine laughed, obviously smitten, while Joel made a clumsy bow and muttered, "How do you do?"

Ginjevine made an attempt to recover herself, her husband scowling at her. She folded her hands again. "Tell me, Joel, what grade are you in?"

"Eight," came the reply, "beginning next year."

"Ah. I assume you're giving thought to boarding school, then."

Joel sent a perplexed look at Joy, who lifted her head and replied for him. "No," she said smoothly, "boarding school is out of the question."

Mr. Caudell snorted.

Ginjevine was clearly shocked. "Whatever do you mean? Surely you realize how important a good preparatory school is."

Joy took a deep breath, aware that Weston had rocked forward onto his toes, his hands balled into fists at his sides. "We have good schools right here in Folly Creek," she explained patiently. "Joel has never thought of going anywhere else, and I've never thought of sending him away. Besides, we can't afford it." From the looks on their faces, she knew she had done the unpardonable: she had mentioned money. But, if it hadn't been that, it would have been something else. She sighed and let it go, sensing the futility.

"Actually, Joel's grades are quite impressive," Weston said a bit too loudly. "His teachers think he's wonderful. And, boy, you ought to see him swing a bat!"

"I'm sure," Mr. Caudell muttered, turning away his head, and Weston seemed to give up and relax all at once. Joy could see that he was angry, but she also saw that he was very much in control. He rubbed the back of his head with one hand, the other going to his waist.

"Oh, I forgot," he said cryptically, "you wouldn't have anything to compare it with. After all, you never saw Parker or me play ball, did you, Father?"

Calvin Caudell's fine brows rose in tandem. He cleared his throat again and stood up. "I think it's time we were going." He held out his hand to his wife. "My dear."

Ginjevine set her mouth against what seemed a protest and laid her hand in his, rising smoothly to her feet. "So nice to have met you," she said smoothly. "We really must run."

"Yes, of course," Weston said tersely. "I'll walk you to your car."

"Don't bother," the elder Caudell murmured dismissively, but Weston had no intention of being put off.

"Not at all, Father. I wouldn't have it any other way." He clapped Joel on the shoulder affectionately. "Listen, chum, I'd be grateful if you'd make some iced tea. My throat is parched."

The boy knew he was being gotten out of the way, but he took the hint without comment. In fact, he did them both proud. He nodded politely at the Caudells and then pulled himself quite erect. "I'm very glad to meet you at last," he said evenly. "Goodbye." And he turned on his heel and left the room.

Joy felt like applauding him, and Mrs. Caudell seemed rather affected herself. Her hands began to flutter in a surprisingly emotional manner. "Goodbye," she said, one hand slipping beneath her husband's elbow.

"Goodbye," Joy returned, rising by rote to see them to the door.

Weston instantly intercepted her, however. "Never mind, hon," he said gently. "I'm sure Joel could use your help with that tea. I won't be a minute." And to her absolute amazement, he slipped an arm about her waist and kissed her firmly on the mouth. She was still riveted to that spot, her jaws clamped in shock, when the door closed behind him, his parents preceding him out.

"Disgusting display!" she heard Calvin Caudell say as he left her porch.

"Life in general seems to disgust you, Father," Weston commented smoothly, his voice gradually receding.

Joy closed her eyes and sighed. Well, what had he expected? she wondered. Had he really pinned his hopes on this meeting? He must have known how it would turn out. On the other hand, Ginjevine Caudell had seemed taken by her grandson despite herself. Perhaps Weston had counted on that maternal instinct to surface in Joel's case, but why include her in this when his parents' reactions had been a foregone conclusion?

Joel came into the room, inquiring sheepishly, "Are they gone?"

She nodded. "Wes is walking them to their car."

He slipped his hands into the pockets of his pants. "It's funny," he said pensively, "but they're not at all what I expected. I mean, I guess I thought she'd have warts and be riding a broom, you know? I don't know what I thought he'd be like. The king of Russia maybe." He shrugged.

"Russia doesn't have a king," she told him laughingly, but his attention went suddenly to the window as Weston's voice came to them, loud and angry.

"Don't be absurd!" he was saying. "You already have my answer!"

Joy and Joel looked at one another, worry and curiosity overwhelming all else. Suddenly Joel ran to the couch and peered out the window. An instant later, he lifted the sash, blatantly eavesdropping. Joy opened her mouth to scold, then closed it again and hurried over to join him. Their own lives were involved here, after all. Joel moved over to make room for her.

Ginjevine Caudell was playing peacemaker, her slender hands placed as restraints on the arms of her son and husband. She appeared to be pleading quietly with her husband, but Calvin Caudell was shaking his head in seething indignation.

"It's abominable!" he replied to whatever she had said. "How can he do this to us? Wasn't it bad enough that his brother turned his back on all we stand for?"

"Parker didn't turn his back on anyone!" Weston interjected. "You turned your back on him! All Parker ever wanted to do was lead his own life, and that's what you couldn't stand! It didn't have anything to do with Cynthia or social position or even family responsibility. It had to do with your need to call all the shots, to feel superior to everyone else!"

"Weston!" Ginjevine Caudell was clearly appalled by her son's straight talk. Calvin was incensed.

"You ingrate! After all I've done for you!"

"Do you really want to do something for me, Father?" Weston demanded. "Something that really matters? Then accept that boy in there as your grandson!"

Joel turned a stricken face to Joy. It was clear from that one horrified expression that he blamed himself for what was happening out there. She squeezed his shoulder, silently telling him that he was wrong.

"You can't blackmail me!" Calvin Caudell bawled, and his wife shrieked, jerking their attention back to the window. The elder man shook his wife's hand from his arm and for the first time seemed genuinely bent on physical assault, his hands knotted into fists.

"Calvin, no!"

He seemed not even to hear her, but he did not strike. "You can drop the family account!" he told his son. "You can disavow your inheritance, break your mother's heart, but you'll not cow me!"

Weston stood toe to toe with him, shouting his reply. "Break my mother's heart? Good God, man, how can you expect her to be anything but heartbroken when you insist upon turning your back on your own flesh and blood? That's what you're doing, Father, and that's what you're asking me to do!"

"No such thing!" the old man blustered. "I warned him! I warned Parker what the outcome would be if he insisted on marrying that Cynthia woman! I told him I couldn't countenance the issue of such an ill-suited match! It's his fault!"

"Whoever's fault it is," Weston yelled, "it's not Joel's, and I won't turn my back on him! And I won't live my life as if everyone I come in contact with is after the Caudell fortune!"

"Please!" Ginjevine had just about reached her breaking point. She dropped her head to her hands. "Stop this, please!"

Joy turned her face away from the awful scene, embarrassed and ashamed for all of them. Suddenly Joel leapt up and hit the door, throwing it wide and bolting through. Stunned, Joy made to follow, but good sense told her that her presence might well add fuel to the fire. Torn, she turned back to the window in time to see Joel fling his arms around his uncle's waist. Weston quieted at once, his full attention going to the boy. He bent toward him, speaking quickly. Joy caught the words "house" and "sorry" and she knew from the way Joel's shoulders heaved that he was sobbing. She tore away from the scene and ran out onto the porch. There, perched upon the step, she was halted by what she was seeing. Ginjevine Caudell had lifted her face from her hands and walked timidly toward the boy. Even as Joy watched, she was gently turning his face up. Her trembling fingers touched his face, drying his tears.

"Oh, my dear," she said, and a little push from Weston sent the boy right into her arms. "Calvin," she implored, "he's so like Parker!" Weston rocked back on his heels, his arms swinging around behind him, one hand rolling into a fist and slamming into the open palm of the other.

Joy stepped back, watching with a mixture of elation and despondency. Calvin Caudell tugged at his collar, cleared his throat, and looked down at his grandson. After a moment a grimace twisted his face.

"It was never the boy!" Mr. Caudell said in a loud, gravelly voice. "I always meant to accept him one day. It was the principle! We all have our place in the world. Some are meant for one thing, others for another. That's the problem in a nutshell! And I'm sorry, Weston, but the woman is wholly unsuitable."

The woman is... Joy's hand went to her throat. Well, it was only what she'd expected, what she'd known. Joel just might be acceptable, after all, but the woman, Joy herself—as Cynthia before her—could never hope to be deemed suitable. Never.

She backed up and leaned against the doorjamb for support, telling herself that her struggle was not for nothing. Joel's position had changed; Weston had seen to that, and how right he had been to do so. It was a masterful stroke of genius, getting them here to meet the boy. Apparently he'd even risked his own position within the family, but it had worked—for Joel. Doors of all sorts had just opened for the boy, doors that once had seemed closed forever. It was enough, more than she'd hoped for—even if it meant giving him up, giving up both of them.

Weston was saying something about love being love and how it didn't pay attention to silly things like social status and money and snobbery, but Joy was no longer really listening. His words were background noise above which the voice inside her head was detailing what she must do.

While Weston and his father continued to argue in less volatile tones, Ginjevine Caudell was getting to know her grandson. The two of them stood a little apart, talking quietly but animatedly. Some part of Joy noted nostalgically that the boy was almost as tall as his grandmother, who was smiling softly, her hands folded almost in an attitude of prayer.

Presently Mr. Caudell stormed off in a huff and got into the back seat of the limo. The chauffeur leapt up and hurried around to hold the door even though Mr. Caudell was already inside. Ginjevine cast an anxious eye over her shoulder, primly kissed her grandson on the cheek, and hurried toward the car, waving at Weston. The chauffeur put her inside and closed the door decorously, then turned and walked around to the driver's side, got in and started the engine.

As the long black car moved away, Weston walked over to slip an arm about the boy's shoulders. Joel hugged him, and together they turned toward the house.

For just a moment Joy stayed where she was, watching with tear-filled eyes, silently celebrating the great affection that had grown between these two, even knowing now what it meant for her. Then she turned and hurried inside. By the time they strolled into the house, she was in the kitchen, peering into the refrigerator, as if contemplating dinner.

Joel muttered that his shoes were killing his feet and slipped away. Weston ambled over to the sink. Joy was very aware of him, terribly so.

"Let's go out to dinner," he said with sudden exuberance. "I feel like celebrating."

"Nonsense," she managed, raising up from the vegetable drawer with a head of cauliflower. "You're probably dying for a home cooked meal."

He laughed. "I am at that."

"Well then," she said brightly, "let me welcome you home in proper style." She smiled at him, determined to behave as if all was well and settled. He stayed where he was, leaning against the counter as she began to wash the cauliflower. After a bit he reached out a hand and smoothed her hair. She felt a tingle everywhere he touched.

"You were marvelous just now," he told her quietly, but she protested, shaking her head.

"I haven't done anything." Mentally she added, *yet*.

"Not truc. I don't know of any other woman who could have handled the situation more graciously. I'm just sorry about the way I had to do this. It was worth it, though. It went much better than you probably realize."

"I'm glad," she said, smiling at him, and suddenly he moved forward, his arms coming around her.

"It's so good to be home," he whispered into her hair, and she stood very still, just letting him hold her. After a bit, she moved away a little.

"You haven't had time to relax," she said. "Why don't we all get comfortable? You go and change, and when you get back, dinner will be well underway. All right?"

"Perfect," he said, "but first..." He drew her to him, wet hands and all, and kissed her long and lovingly, his hands moving over her back, fitting her body to his in that way she found so wildly arousing. When he finally released her, she was close to tears, but she managed to smile and hold them at bay. "See you soon," he told her, moving away. She nodded, dry-eyed and serene, holding the tears for harder times yet to come.

"Soon," she said, making it a promise to herself, a vow—for all their sakes. He smiled and left her, not knowing that she meant it to be one of their last times together.

Lee Jackson's decision to finish college planted the seed in her mind, but it was not until she saw the notice in the newspaper about an increase in local college funding for tuition that she was able to summon the courage to begin. It was a perfect plan.

She had attended college until Cynthia had died and had only dropped out because she had realized how difficult it would be to continue with her education while also caring for Joel and working full-time. She had always meant to go back to school, and she'd said as much to Joel on more than one occasion.

The article gave her the ideal lead-in. She folded the paper back on itself, exposing the one-inch column, and laid it on the kitchen counter. By the time Joel came in from the tree house, she knew exactly what she was going to say.

"Did you read this?" she asked, picking up the paper. He turned to look over his shoulder, reaching for the refrigerator door handle in the same convoluted motion.

"Naw, I just read the funnies."

She knew that, of course, but she let it pass without comment, concentrating instead on the newspaper in her hand. "It says here that they've gotten additional funding for student aid at the college. I wonder if I ought to reapply? What do you think?"

Joel shrugged, then bent to peer into the refrigerator. "Might as well if you want to." It came out muffled as he was speaking directly into a milk carton. He straightened with it, closed the refrigerator and went to the cabinet for a glass. "You still want to go back to college?"

"Why not?" she asked innocently. "It would be pretty tough. I'd have to work part-time, drive over the mountain and back every day, but I expect Wes would help out."

"Sure he would." He took a long drink, wiped his mouth on the back of his hand, and walked over to sit down at the table without bothering to put the milk carton away.

Joy sat down opposite him, ignoring the open milk carton and the smear on the back of his hand. She chose her words carefully, delivering them with great ease. "You wouldn't mind spending more time with Wes, would you?"

He shrugged again. "Heck, no."

"You already spend a great deal of time with him. I mean, between the time he spends here and the time you spend over there, you practically live together. Have you ever thought of that, living with Weston?"

He looked her square in the eye. "Not really. I thought I might have to one day when I first met him, but it was too scary to really think about back then."

"Would you mind living with Weston?" she asked, her voice getting smaller despite her best efforts.

Again he gave her that frank look. "It'd be all right," he said, "if that's what you want."

She had to look away then in order to keep her voice steady. "Would you be hurt if I did?"

He took a long moment to reply, his tumbler of milk warming in his hands. "You mean, so you could go back to college?"

She cocked her head to one side, proceeding very carefully. "It might be my last opportunity. I'm not getting any younger, you know, and with Weston's help, well, it might just be too good to pass up." She made herself smile and lift her shoulders. "It's just an idea. Maybe I'll talk to Wes about it, see what he thinks."

He nodded and lifted his glass. "That's a good idea." Apparently unshaken, he drained the milk in one long drink, set the glass on the table, rose and went out with a smile. Joy didn't even mind cleaning up after him for once. She put the milk away, then rinsed the glass and put it in the drainer. She wondered if the second step would be as easy to take.

It was Sunday afternoon before she could bring herself to find out. In the meantime she concentrated on keeping busy and behaving as normally as possible. She made no effort to avoid Weston, but she did manage to be constantly engaged with some urgent project whenever he was around. Over the weekend she cleaned out the kitchen cabinets, mended a basketful of clothes, and moved the furniture around in nearly every room of the house. She could tell that all this activity aggravated him, but he seemed to temper his impatience, helping out as much as he could and not pressing the issue when she artfully avoided his touch. By Sunday, however, with church and dinner and the cleaning up out of the way, she had run out of diversions, and so finally took the bull by the horns.

"Has Joel said anything to you about me maybe going back to school?" she asked as they sat down on the living room sofa.

Weston gave her a surprised look. "No. Should he have?"

She shrugged. "Not really. It's just that I've always wanted to and lately I've been considering it."

"And you've discussed it with him?"

She nodded. "The idea doesn't seem to bother him in the least. Before you and he became so close, I worried that he would feel abandoned or threatened if I concentrated on college, but now..." She stopped, letting him draw his own conclusions. "It would be difficult working, driving back and forth over the mountain in all kinds of weather, homework, studying. I'm not sure I'm up to it, frankly."

He covered her hand with his. "Of course you are! Don't sell yourself short. You can do anything you really want to. Besides, Joel and I will help. You know we will."

She smiled at him. It was so easy to do. He was so good, so kind and generous. She wondered now how she had ever feared him, suspected his motives, distrusted her own feelings about him. She took an odd pride in knowing the kind of man Weston Caudell really was, but with the pride came a certain sadness, a great, deep regret for what could not be—for his sake and for Joel's.

"I'll have to think about this some more," she told him, "kick it around in my head a while longer."

He put his arm around her. "You do that. Just remember that Joel and I are behind you, whatever you decide."

Behind her. She made her smile stay in place, made the tears wait, willed her muscles to remain relaxed and unresponsive to the inner tension she felt. He and Joel were behind her—or would be. He didn't know how prophetic those words were, for the time was coming when she would have to put them, Weston and Joel and her love for them both, behind her once and for all.

Chapter Ten

For more than a week she kept the matter of returning to college an open issue. She made a point of saying, "If I go back to school" or "Should I go back to school" as a preface for nearly every remark, and she made a point, too, of letting Mr. Ball know that she was seriously considering leaving his employ. He was shocked at first and then supportive but fretful about losing her, and she felt it only right that he should be the first to know this thing was going to happen. She told him on Friday, giving her two-week notice and allowing herself the weekend to make her full intentions known to Weston and Joel.

Just contemplating what she had to do was terribly difficult for her, and for the first time since she'd brought the matter up, she let it drop, saying nothing on Saturday or even Sunday until well into the evening—and then she waited almost until the last moment. They had rented a video and had watched it together at Weston's house. Wes had popped a tubful of popcorn for the occasion and laid in plenty of Joel's favorite soft drink. They'd gorged on popcorn and root beer, skipping a proper dinner this once, to Joel's delight. The movie had played out and was rewinding while they watched the evening news and gathered empty pop bottles to be returned to the store. Joel stretched on the couch, yawned and announced that he was ready to get some shut-eye. Joy knew it was as good a lead-in as she was bound to get.

"Why don't you just sack out here?" she suggested. "I'm sure Wes won't mind. There's plenty of space."

"I don't mind at all," Weston said smoothly. "Why don't you take the room next to mine? I've always sort of thought of it as yours anyway."

"And tomorrow," Joy blurted cheerily, "I'll bring over some of your things, sort of make it official, you know?"

They both looked at her as if she'd just delivered the Gettysburg address in Swedish. She herself felt as if her grasp on the moment was tenuous. She smiled awkwardly and sat down on Weston's coffee table. Weston looked up at her from his place on the floor, his back to the sofa where Joel rose up on one elbow to stare, his young brow puckered. Joy placed the empty bottles on the floor between her feet and tried to get a grip.

"I didn't mean to say it that way," she began. "It's just that, well, you both know I've been thinking about the future, *my* future, and I've worked this whole thing out in my head now. It's simple really, thanks to you, Wes, because I couldn't even dream of getting back to college if you weren't here for Joel, if I didn't know you'd take such excellent care of him." She looked down, unable to meet Joel's eyes squarely with what she had to say next. "Joel, you know how much Wes loves you and how much I love you, too, and the truth is that Weston is in a much better position to take care of you than I am. I'm too young, Joel, to be guardian of such a grown-up boy like you, and it would be so hard, working at Ball's, studying, driving over the mountain continuously. Really, when you think about it, this is the best solution for everyone. Really."

She couldn't go on until she'd swallowed down the thick lump that had come up in her throat. She paused a moment longer to take in a clean breath while the impact of all she'd said made itself known. Joel was the first to get it and the first to speak.

"You want me to move in with Uncle Wes," he said flatly, and Joy looked up, smiling gently.

"It's really the only way, sweetie. Unless I'm to take the next ten years getting my degree. And I won't be so far away, really, just over the mountain. We'll see each other so often you won't even think about my not being here."

He lay down on the couch without comment, as if trying to feel what it would be like to be there without her. She took a deep breath and clasped her hands together to stop their trembling. After a long moment Weston spoke.

"I didn't realize you were thinking like this," he said haltingly. "I knew you were contemplating going back to school but... Isn't moving away quite a large leap from taking a few part-time courses?"

"Well, it began like that," she lied, "but the more I thought about it the more I realized there was nothing holding me back from going full-time—as long as Joel's with you."

He got up from the floor, practically bolting up with only the slightest hitch in the flow of motion. At once he began to pace, his attitude one of growing anger held carefully in check.

"You'll have to forgive me if I'm having a little trouble with this. It's just that I haven't been thinking in terms of Joel and me without you!"

"That's funny," she said deliberately. "I thought that was exactly what you wanted, at least in the beginning."

"We all wanted different things in the beginning!" he exploded. "But that doesn't justify you suddenly picking up and moving over the mountain!"

"Why not?" she demanded, getting to her feet. "How long did you think about it before you pulled up stakes and moved in here?" He glared at her wordlessly, and she squared her shoulders. "What I'm doing makes better sense than what you did," she said. "You didn't even know what you were getting into. You didn't know us, and we didn't know you, but you did what you thought was best, and it turned out all right. That's all I'm trying to do—that's exactly what I'm trying to do."

She held her breath, her throat thick with tears again. Weston stared at her as if he was trying to read her mind, then sighed and twisted about and sighed again.

"All right!" he blurted finally. "Move over the mountain if that's what you want. And don't worry about us! Just don't give us a second thought!"

"I won't," she told him tremulously. "Why should I when everything's working out so fine? You've found each other, and Joel's even told me how he thinks of you almost as a father. Your parents are even coming around. Why, one day soon you're all going to be one big happy family—as you should be. And I... I'll have my degree. Imagine that! Me, the high-school drop-out with a college degree. Life's so... Isn't life just so..." She couldn't make herself say one more word.

She turned suddenly and grabbed up her purse, holding it tight against her middle. On wobbly legs she moved to the couch, stooped, and brushed back the bangs that fell across Joel's forehead. He would soon need a haircut. For some reason he always hated to have his hair cut. Why did little boys do that? But then he wasn't so little anymore. He didn't need anyone to hold his hand and tell him not to be frightened. He needed someone who could show him how to be a man. He needed Weston and his grandparents. He needed family, real family. He did not need her. Perhaps he didn't know it yet, but he would soon.

She kissed his forehead, rose, and walked briskly away. She told herself that the most difficult part of her plan was over. Everything else would be a snap compared with what she had just done.

She knew it was true, but somehow it didn't make her feel any better.

Getting through the next two weeks took every ounce of strength and courage Joy possessed. To the outside world she presented a smiling, confident face and lied with more grace and ease than she had ever imagined she could. In reality, however, she constantly teetered on the verge of tears. Every moment was a battle to maintain composure, a misery in and of itself, wearing her down, sapping her energy so that she collapsed into bed at night, beaten, morose and often sobbing until exhaustion brought respite.

She took to sleeping in Cynthia's room, too tired and dispirited to climb the ladder to her attic. Invariably she thought of the evening she'd spent here in Weston's arms. At first, it was sheer agony to recall, but in a strange way the memories began to comfort her, their bittersweet sharpness more real to her than anything else in her life at the moment. She began to dwell on other rich memories of her life with Joel and Cynthia. She found a great deal to treasure, and that helped to make life at the moment bearable, that and the knowledge that by bowing out she had secured the future for Joel and Weston.

The most difficult thing was to play out her assigned role in the presence of one or the other of them. For his part Joel seemed content enough, if somewhat muddled. She packed up his things and began taking them to Weston's house, hoping to make the transition as gradual and painless as possible. She made a point of being cheery and optimistic during those little visits, pleading that she had a million things to do when he complained that she didn't stay long enough and then holding herself firmly in check when the next moment he ran out to play as if she would be there always at his convenience. It was gut-wrenching every time she left him, but she had her memories and the sure knowledge that she was doing what was best for him.

Weston, however, was another matter. As he had so often during their entire acquaintance, he puzzled her. She knew that he was glad to have Joel with him at last, and she had expected that having instigated the move herself would spare him any feelings of guilt at accomplishing his goal. Yet, whenever she saw him, he invariably failed to meet her eye, tending instead to stare off into space or to busy himself with something else as if she weren't really there at all. She realized at some point that she had unconsciously supposed he would feel grateful toward her for having given up Joel, but she saw no evidence of anything resembling gratitude in his cool aloofness. It was, as usual, impossible for her to know what he was feeling or thinking, but she trusted that eventually his good sense would tell him she had done the right thing for everyone. The old way, the unofficial sharing of the boy they both cherished, would only have grown more complicated as time wore on.

That much seemed certain, especially when she considered her own feelings for Weston. As mystifying as he was, she could not help finding much to admire in him. He had kept track of Joel for years, trusting Cynthia to care for him, sublimating his own instinct to know his brother's son, and surfacing only when he felt the boy might need him. Moreover, once his suspicions about her as a guardian had been put to rest, he had exhibited unusual patience. He had, in effect, uprooted his life, risked disinheritance and financial failure, and endured what must seem for so sophisticated and privileged a man a kind of backwater existence simply to share in the boy's life. He had been generous. He had deferred to her authority in instances that must have galled him severely. He had included her in his plans for activities with Joel. And despite the physical attraction that had developed between them, he had not pressured her. Was it any wonder that she had fallen in love with him?

But that way led to disaster. Perhaps if the Caudells had remained out of the picture they could have shared something together other than their concern for Joel. Yet, it was better for both Joel and Weston that their individual relationships with the senior Caudells be normalized and, if possible, enriched. It was because she saw that happening that she could go on.

Twice during the first week she walked into Weston's house to find Joel talking animatedly on the telephone with his newly acquainted grandparents, who, having capitulated at last, seemed intent on making up for lost time. Like most youngsters, all it took for Joel to warm up to them was an expression of genuine interest. The differences of the past had been eliminated—and she with them, but it did not seem too exorbitant a price to pay if it meant happiness for those she loved best.

Things were, in fact, moving quite rapidly on the Caudell front. It seemed that Mr. and Mrs. Caudell wanted their grandson to visit them in their home quite soon. They proposed, in fact, to entertain him for an entire month, but Joel was uncertain that he wanted to be away from Folly Creek that long. They began to negotiate a shorter stay. Eventually they settled upon a two-week sojourn and began to debate a favorable date for the visit to commence.

Convinced that she had done the right thing, Joy pressed ahead, visiting Mr. Kincaid as the next step. She laid it out for the lawyer as calmly and rationally as she could. Weston had turned out to be an able, caring, intelligent man with a genuine love for his nephew. The two had become quite close. He had engineered a reconciliation between the boy and his grandparents. His financial means far outstripped her own. In short, she was convinced that Joel belonged with his uncle. As for herself, she had decided to go back to college, secure in the knowledge that Joel was receiving the very best of care.

"And I'm convinced," she concluded, "that the arrangements I've made should be official."

Kincaid rocked back in his creaky chair and templed his fingers. "In other words," he said, "you want me to draw up papers transferring your guardianship of the boy to his uncle."

She nodded, overcome for the moment by the enormity of what she was doing, and blinked back tears. "It's tough for me to admit it, but he belongs with Weston. They belong together. They're a family."

Kincaid stared at her long and hard. "This Weston Caudell's really won you over, hasn't he? But what about you? You love that boy."

"Very much," she admitted, "so much that I want only what's best for him."

"And you're genuinely convinced that it's best for him to be with his uncle?"

"Absolutely," she said, holding her chin aloft. Kincaid pursed his lips and toyed with a pencil, obviously considering all she'd said and done since she'd entered his office, comparing it, no doubt, with her previous visits. Finally he seemed to reach a decision. He sat forward and folded his long, knobby arms over the blotter on his desk.

"All right," he said. "Papers'll be ready in a few days."

Joy's relief was tempered with a great sadness, a deepening of her sense of loss, but she managed a wan smile. They chatted a moment about what she intended to study, discussing the various pros and cons of several different majors. Then Joy rose and left, one step closer to severing her last tie with the Caudells.

That evening was particularly difficult, so much so that she did not go over to Weston's but chose instead to call him on the phone and tell him what she'd done. She managed to impart the news in a fairly reasonable tone, shedding silent, unseen tears in the process. He was brusque and cold and at one point sounded actually incredulous.

"You've done *what*?"

She closed her eyes and gripped the receiver so hard her knuckles turned white. "It's the only sensible thing to do," she managed. "What if there's a medical emergency of some sort? They won't treat him without the consent of a guardian. Would you want to wait until you could reach me and I could drive over the mountain to get here? I'm just thinking of Joel."

"Are you?" he accused. "Or are you just thinking of yourself? You know, Joy, if you don't want to be with me, all you have to do is say so. You don't have to cut this boy's world in half!"

She was too stunned for a moment to speak, but then what was there to say that wouldn't make matters worse? "I—it won't be that way for very long. He has you, and he has his grandparents now, thanks to you."

There came a long silence ended, finally, by a sigh. "If I ever figure you out... But I suppose it's a little late for that."

"Could we stick to the subject?" she asked shakily. "I'll let you know when the papers are ready. We can sign them at Kincaid's office. And, Wes, don't you think it would be better if we didn't mention this to Joel? I don't want too many changes coming at him at once."

The reply that brought seemed to come from way out in left field. "I asked you this once before," he said. "Now I'm asking again: does this have anything to do with Lee Jackson Goode?"

Joy went rigid and closed her eyes, hating herself for what she was about to do. "In a way. It was Lee who got me started thinking about college. He's going back, too."

"How very convenient," he snapped.

She forced a cheerful voice. "Yes, isn't it? It will be nice to have a friend on campus."

"A friend," he repeated cryptically. "Well, if your friend and a college education are what you want—" He broke off, sighing, and she could sense the struggle he was having with himself. Finally, he came back on. "I don't know what to say or do anymore," he admitted haltingly. "As usual, you are calling the shots. I don't have to like it, but I'll go along with whatever you want."

"Thank you," she whispered weakly. "I—I'll let you know when." She waited a moment, but he said nothing more, so she told him goodbye and hung up. This was supposed to be getting easier, she reminded herself. When, dear God, was this going to start getting easier? She just sat there by the telephone, numb and hurting all at the same time, until it was dark enough to go to bed.

Joel left Folly Creek the next Friday morning in a chauffeur-driven limousine to spend two weeks with his grandparents. Fortunately, he did not know what, that very afternoon, was to transpire concerning his guardianship, and so he thought only of the new experiences awaiting him. As he requested, Joy was there to see him off. It was a moment she had never expected to come, and she couldn't help wondering what Cynthia would have thought of all this. She was glad that Cynthia had never been placed in her own position, but she had to believe that Cynthia would have done exactly what she was doing or at least that Cynthia would have understood her actions, especially as Weston obviously did not.

He was civil in so far as he actually muttered a greeting when she arrived. Otherwise, he stood stiffly with his hands in his pockets, trying to look as if he were unaware of her presence. He stood apart while she chatted with Joel, admonished him to behave and hugged him goodbye, then he stepped in at the last minute to ruffle the boy's hair and tell him to have a good time. He turned away as soon as the car door was closed and strode across the lawn to the house, where he stood in the doorway, gazing out at the retreating vehicle as if his only reason to live had just gone with it. She wanted desperately to go to him, to take his face in her hands and smooth his troubled brow, but what then? They could never go back to the old arrangement, not now that the Caudells were in the picture. That would only cause him more trouble in the long run, as she well knew. She turned and walked down the street toward town and her last day at Ball's.

For once she wanted the day to go slowly, to crawl along one long moment after another, for at day's end her new life would begin, and it looked to be a lonely, bare existence. All that would remain was the actual move, and she already planned to spend the following day looking for an apartment near the university. It wouldn't be anything special, of course, because she could afford only the bare necessities, and even at that she would have to find another job quickly, but none of that mattered. She would get on with it somehow.

If she'd expected that knowledge to make it easier, however, she was far too optimistic. Just leaving Ball's was much more difficult than she'd imagined. Mrs. Ball came in to say goodbye with her husband, and there were several regular customers who stopped in to say their farewells and wish her success. Mr. Ball presented her with a handsome book satchel and made her promise to visit whenever she was in town. Pritikin Marsh and his wife stopped in to say that they were sponsoring a social after the next church meeting in her honor. Preacher Marsh even took a moment to speak to her in privacy, telling her that while he believed Weston Caudell to be a fine man he had never questioned her fitness to serve as Joel's guardian.

"I'm sorry it's turned out this way," he said, "and I want you to know that I for one recognize the sacrifice you're making."

She could only say that she didn't blame him for anything and that Joel's happiness was reward enough. It was all, she told him, for the best.

"Things do have a way of working out," he said, "and I'm sure they'll work out for you."

She asked him to serve as her ears and eyes in her absence, much as he'd done for Weston. He agreed without hesitation. Afterward she felt better able to face Mr. Kincaid and Weston.

The preacher and his wife gave her a ride over to Kincaid's office and left her there with a parting wave. It seemed fitting somehow that Pritikin Marsh should deliver her to this meeting. She wondered if Weston would agree, but that was another in a long list of things she would likely never know. Meanwhile the moment awaited. Weston's Suburban was parked across the street, which meant that he was already in Kincaid's office. Steeling herself, she pushed open the heavy, old-fashioned wood and beveled glass door. In the past, passing through this sturdy, solid door had comforted her, but not today. As she climbed the narrow stairway to the office that comprised the second floor of this little building, she felt the heat rising from the dry cleaners below and heard the constant hum of the air conditioner that Kincaid ran all summer long.

At the top of the stairs she opened another door, a hollow, nondescript one bare of paint and stained with fingerprints. Beyond it was a small outer office where, as far as Joy knew, no secretary or receptionist had ever sat. Kincaid was there now, his long, lean frame bending over the small desk piled high with correspondence and file folders, a telephone receiver trapped between shoulder and jaw. He flashed her an apologetic glance and went back to digging into the piles on the desk. After a rather frantic moment, he found what he was looking for, a document of some sort, spoke to the person on the other end of the line and flipped through the pages.

"Aw," he said speaking into the phone, "I was right. There. Double-checked and verified. I have clients waiting." After a pause he said, "No trouble at all. Part of the job. Take care now." He hung up and smiled at Joy compassionately. He opened his arms, their span encompassing almost the whole of the room. "This way," he said in his deep, lawyerly tones.

Joy preceded him into the inner office. It was a bit roomier than the outer one but not by much, especially with Weston Caudell taking up his share of space. He rose as she came in, his expression glum and very nearly hostile. He gave her a spare nod and turned away. Kincaid filled the strained silence with copious throat-clearing.

"You two know each other," he said, "so we'll dispense with the formal introductions." He motioned for Joy to take her usual place and folded himself into his own cracked leather chair, crossing his long legs and bringing his hands together. "I expect you both know what's at stake here," he said, "so I'll keep the sermonizing to a minimum. Now, Joy, you're the legal guardian, designated by the actual parent before her passing, of a boy child, age 13, named Joel Parker Caudell. Is it your intention, here and now, to relinquish said guardianship?"

"It is," she answered in a tiny, strained voice, her hands tightly clutching the strap of her purse as it rested in her lap.

Kincaid nodded and pivoted toward Weston. "You, Mr. Caudell, are the uncle of Joel Parker Caudell, and as such you're willing and able to take over the care and guardianship of the child. Is that correct?"

Weston took a deep breath and let it out again. "That's about the shape of it."

Kincaid brushed lint from his pant leg. "I must ask both of you if this intention to transfer guardianship was developed in the desire to protect the interests of the juvenile, Joel Parker Caudell?"

Joy concentrated on her hands. "It was."

Weston made an agitated movement, crossing his legs and renegotiating his position. "Don't look at me," he said. "This wasn't my idea."

"But you do agree," Kincaid pressed, "that transferring guardianship is in the boy's best interests, do you not?"

"Well, I don't really have much choice," Weston told him. "I mean, I'm not going to let her dump him on some street corner somewhere." Joy sent him an incredulous look, while Kincaid lifted his dark eyebrows.

"That's hardly the attitude I'd expected," the lawyer said reasonably. "I was under the impression that you came to Folly Creek seeking custody of the boy."

"I came seeking to know the boy," Weston shot back, "to make sure that he was getting the kind of care and nurturing he needs and deserves."

"And was he?"

Weston blinked at the lawyer's face, some of the hostility draining out of him, then shrugged and sat up a little straighter. "He was," he stated flatly.

Joy sat very still, unsure of what was happening here. Did he really think she was abandoning Joel? Or did he admit on some level that she was doing what was best? She didn't know what to think, which was par for the course where Weston Caudell was concerned. At any rate, she preferred to leave it to him and Kincaid to conduct this matter. Kincaid seemed to have other ideas.

"Joy, have you explained to Mr. Caudell your reasons for seeking to transfer guardianship?"

She bit the inside of her cheek. "I've tried."

"Mr. Caudell, do you not agree with her reasoning?"

"Sir," he said, "I can't begin to fathom her reasoning."

"Well, well." Kincaid sat forward, reached for a pencil and tucked it behind his ear. "We do not seem to have consensus."

Joy spoke out in alarm. "Is that really necessary, as long as he's willing to accept guardianship and I want to give it to him?"

Kincaid spread his hands. "No, not in the narrow sense. Only in a broad interpretation."

"That's good enough," Joy insisted. "Get on with it."

Kincaid looked to Weston. "Mr. Caudell?"

There came a brief pause, then Weston flipped up a hand. "If that's what she wants..."

Kincaid shook his head and opened the shallow center drawer of his desk. "All right." He withdrew five stapled copies of the legal document. "With both signatures, it ought to be a routine matter. If you'll each take a copy, read it and sign your names in the appropriate places, we'll get this marathon underway." He thumbed two copies off the top and handed one to each of them, then uncapped a couple of pens and handed those over, too.

Joy pretended to read, the words all running together and refusing to make sense, then signed her name with bold, determined strokes and passed that copy to Weston, immediately reaching for another. By the time she reached for the third, she was aware of a hitch in the process. Wes was simply staring at the papers, the pen gripped tightly in his fist. He looked up at her, his eyes wide and smoky and pleading.

"I can't do this," he said, and to her everlasting amazement he stood, dumping the documents onto the floor and dropping the pen atop them. "What in God's name are you trying to do?" he demanded. "This isn't you. You're not this selfish and thoughtless. I just don't get it. You know how much we need you."

Joy sat there looking up at him for several long seconds, his meaning slowly workings its way to clarity. "I know how much you *don't* need me."

He looked at her as if she'd just grown a third eye in the middle of her forehead. "I'd like to know where the hell you got a screwball idea like that," he said.

She didn't know what to say. It was hard to get a grip on herself, to make sense of all this. "You don't need me," she began. "You know you don't need me to...to help you take care of Joel." She licked her lips. "He's not a baby. He...he's happy with you and..." She took a deep breath. "You can give him everything he needs. You have money, a lot of money. Your parents have money and . . ." She sent a desperate look at Kincaid, who merely leaned back and retreated into the role of observer. Clearly he had his own doubts about this arrangement, and until they were satisfied, he wasn't about to try to convince Weston to come around to her point of view. Joy put a hand to her head. How had this all gotten so muddled? It had seemed so clear before.

Weston sat down again, sitting sideways on the armless chair, and took her hands in his. "Will you listen to yourself?" he asked softly. "Since when did money get to be the issue? It didn't mean anything to you before."

"It still doesn't," she replied artlessly, "but why would it? I certainly never had any."

"But I have."

His thumbs lightly rubbing circles on the backs of her hands was proving something of a distraction. Strange how so much heat could be generated by such tiny points of friction. She extracted her hands and folded them primly in her lap.

"Wes," she said reasonably, "you know what your parents think of me. They would never, ever accept me as part of their grandson's life."

"Let alone as part of mine," he said. "Is that what you're getting at?"

She squared her shoulders. "You know what they'll do if you support me, if you press them to accept me."

"You mean they'd disinherit me," he said.

She shrugged. "They did it to Parker."

"I know they did. I also know they suffered and grieved when he died."

"Meaning?"

"Meaning I'm the only son they have left. Meaning they're stubborn and snobbish and foolish at times, but they're not stupid, Joy. They *can* learn from their mistakes. Maybe they would disinherit me, but I don't think so, and even if they did, so what? I don't live off their money. I have money of my own. Parker was just too young to have a secure financial base built up when he married Cynthia, but I'm thirty-five. It's just not a problem."

It all made a surprising kind of sense. Still, it wasn't only money. "What about Joel?" she said. "Do you think he could take being rejected by his grandparents a second time? I don't, not now."

To her surprise, he smiled. "Honey, trust me, that's the last thing that's going to happen. Why do you think I made them come here and meet the boy? I knew that once they'd seen how much like Parker he is they wouldn't be able to resist him. Believe me, they're never going to give up that kid now. Darling, it was all over the minute my mother put her arm around him. After that, it was just a matter of time. And look at them now! I know those two. They're playing the parts of indulgent grandparents right this minute. No, honey, Joel's never going to be without his family again, for better or for worse, I promise. And, Joy, you've got to understand that Joel thinks of you as family. *I* think of you as family. In fact, I thought we were a family, the three of us, or that we would be sooner or later. I'd like sooner, of course, but if you're not sure, if you really don't love me..."

Joy's mouth fell open. In the silence that followed, Kincaid's chair squeaked and he came to his feet. "I believe that's my cue to leave," he said, and immediately left the room.

Joy hardly realized he'd gone. Her heart was working like a team of mules, and the blood seemed to rush through her veins, flooding her cheeks. She knew deep down that in a minute or two she was going to smile or explode or something, but right then she couldn't do anything except stare.

Weston got an endearingly sheepish look on his face, a self-conscious expression that made her want to reach out and slip an arm around his neck, but she just sat, waiting for something she wouldn't even hope for. He went after her hands again and pulled them over onto his lap, turning them palms up in his own.

"I know we never talked about it," he began, "but I intended to. In fact, I intended to do that right after I got my parents down here. Now I admit it looks bad, but honey, if I'd told them first that I wanted to marry you, they'd never have come and I'd have lost my chance to put this family together. I was only trying . . . What?"

The smile she'd been feeling had burst forth and was growing quickly into incredulity. Her hands had left his, had flown up to her cheeks. "You were going to ask me to marry you." It was as much statement as question.

Suddenly he was smiling, too, his eyes a soft bluish gray. "I should have done it right away. I was trying so hard not to spring too much on you at once. I wanted to be patient, you know? And I think I just overshot the mark."

"No," she said, "you didn't. You were just being careful. It was me, all me. I just didn't realize that you're not Parker. You're you, and that makes all the difference."

"But it was me, too," he was saying, "because I should have said right away what was on my mind. It's just that I nearly blew it in the beginning. I thought you were feeling the attraction, too, but then when I first kissed you, well, I realized it wasn't as simple as that. You didn't know who you were dealing with. I had to let you learn to trust me."

"And I did," she insisted. "I was just so confused and frightened of losing Joel to you at first, then I realized how special you are and how much you could suffer if we were together, because of your parents. And when they came, I thought of Parker and all he'd lost because of Cynthia, who was Joel's *mother*, for Pete's sake, and I knew they'd never accept me."

"They don't have to accept you," he told her, "but they will—*if* you have custody of Joel. They'll have to if they're going to maintain contact with their grandson, won't they? And me, too, because I love you and I won't give you up for the Caudells or Lee Jackson Goode or any—"

He never finished it. He didn't have to. For suddenly it was so very clear, so very right and wonderful, not perfect maybe, but with the potential to be perfect. Such potential!

She slipped off the edge of her chair, the doubts and the fears all gone, and threw her arms about his neck. He pulled her onto his lap, and she brought her mouth to his. It seemed that all she'd ever wanted was someone to love, someone to love her, and now here he was, that very special someone, all hers. And Joel's. Hers and Joel's. The three of them. Together. A real family.

Kincaid got a cramp in his foot standing outside the door, waiting for them to come up for air, but he didn't mind, not after what he'd just heard. He liked to have things all wrapped up in a package and tied with a pretty bow, and it wasn't often that it happened, not like this. Pity. The world was a better place when good people settled their differences with love.

And what a settlement! For all of them, for that whole passel of Caudells and even, he figured, for Folly Creek. For what town, what family wouldn't benefit from the alliance of two fine people like these? He and Preacher Marsh had even discussed it between them a time or two, how a loving marriage could solve all the problems, serve all the needs of everyone involved. It was going to be a fine wedding, he reckoned. Everybody in town would be there. Small towns were like that, good ones, anyway, just one big happy family. He smiled at the appropriateness of that particular choice of words, but then it was a family kind of day, a Caudell family kind of day.

* * * * *

COMING NEXT MONTH

#730 BORROWED BABY—Marie Ferrarella
A Diamond Jubilee Book!
Stuck with a six-month-old bundle of joy, reserved policeman Griff Foster became a petrified parent. Then bubbly Liz MacDougall taught him a thing or two about diapers, teething, lullabies and love.

#731 FULL BLOOM—Karen Leabo
When free-spirited Hilary McShane returned early from her vacation, she hadn't expected to find methodical Matthew Burke as a substitute house-sitter. Their life-styles and attitudes clashed, but their love kept growing. . . .

#732 THAT MAN NEXT DOOR—Judith Bowen
New dairy owner Caitlin Forrest was entranced by friendly neighbor Ben Wade. When she discovered that he wanted her farm, however, she wondered exactly how much business he was mixing with pleasure.

#733 HOME FIRES BURNING BRIGHT—Laurie Paige
Book II of HOMEWARD BOUND DUO
Carson McCumber felt he had nothing to offer a woman—especially privileged Tess Garrick. Out to prove the rugged rancher wrong, Tess was determined to keep all the home fires burning. . . .

#734 BETTER TO HAVE LOVED—Linda Varner
Convinced she'd lose, loner Allison Kendall had vowed never to play the game of love. But martial-arts enthusiast Meade Duran was an expert at tearing down all kinds of defenses.

#735 VENUS de MOLLY—Peggy Webb
Cool, controlled banker Samuel Adams became hot under the collar when he thought about his mother marrying Molly Rakestraw's father. But that was before he met the irrepressible Molly!

AVAILABLE THIS MONTH:

#724 CIMARRON KNIGHT
Pepper Adams

#725 FEARLESS FATHER
Terry Essig

#726 FAITH, HOPE and LOVE
Geeta Kingsley

#727 A SEASON FOR HOMECOMING
Laurie Paige

#728 FAMILY MAN
Arlene James

#THE SEDUCTION OF ANNA
Brittany Young

A duo by Laurie Paige

There's no place like home—and Laurie Paige's delightful duo captures that heartwarming feeling in two special stories set in Arizona ranchland. Share the poignant homecomings of two lovely heroines—half sisters Lainie and Tess—as they travel on the road to romance with their rugged, handsome heroes.

A SEASON FOR HOMECOMING—Lainie and Dev's story...available now.

HOME FIRES BURNING BRIGHT—Tess and Carson's story...coming in July.

Come home to A SEASON FOR HOMECOMING (#727) and HOME FIRES BURNING BRIGHT (#733)...only from Silhouette Romance!

A SEASON FOR HOMECOMING (#727) is available now at your favorite retail outlet or order your copy by sending your name, address, and zip or postal code along with a check or money order for $2.25, plus 75¢ postage and handling, payable to Silhouette Reader Service to:

In the U.S.	In Canada
901 Fuhrmann Blvd.	P.O. Box 609
P.O. Box 1396	Fort Erie, Ontario
Buffalo, NY 14269-1396	L2A 5X3

Please specify book title with your order.

HB-1A

Take 4 bestselling love stories FREE

Plus get a FREE surprise gift!

Special Limited-time Offer

Mail to Silhouette Reader Service®

In the U.S.
901 Fuhrmann Blvd.
P.O. Box 1867
Buffalo, N.Y. 14269-1867

In Canada
P.O. Box 609
Fort Erie, Ontario
L2A 5X3

YES! Please send me 4 free Silhouette Romance® novels and my free surprise gift. Then send me 6 brand-new novels every month, which I will receive months before they appear in bookstores. Bill me at the already low price of $2.25* each. There are no shipping, handling or other hidden costs. I understand that accepting these books and gifts places me under no obligation ever to buy any books. I can always return a shipment and cancel at any time. Even if I never buy another book from Silhouette, the 4 free books and the surprise gift are mine to keep forever.

* Offer slightly different in Canada—$2.25 per book plus 69¢ per shipment for delivery.

Sales tax applicable in N.Y. and Iowa. 315 BPA 8178 (CAN)

215 BPA HAYY (US)

Name (PLEASE PRINT)

Address Apt. No.

City State/Prov. Zip/Postal Code

This offer is limited to one order per household and not valid to present Silhouette Romance® subscribers. Terms and prices are subject to change.

© 1990 Harlequin Enterprises Limited

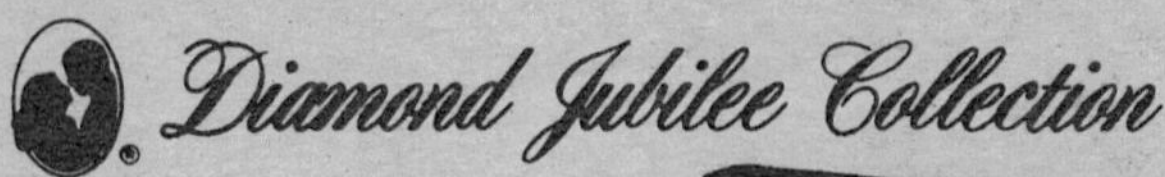

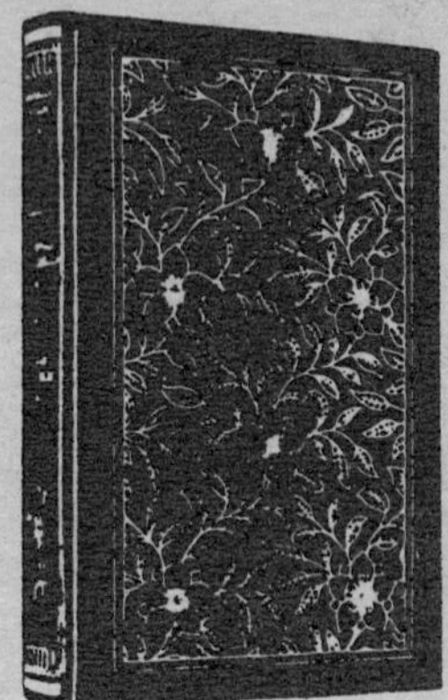

It's our 10th Anniversary... and *you* get a present!

This collection of early Silhouette Romances features novels written by three of your favorite authors:

ANN MAJOR—*Wild Lady*
ANNETTE BROADRICK—*Circumstantial Evidence*
DIXIE BROWNING—*Island on the Hill*

* **These Silhouette Romance titles were first published in the early 1980s and have not been available since!**
* **Beautiful Collector's Edition bound in antique green simulated leather to last a lifetime!**
* **Embossed in gold on the cover and spine!**

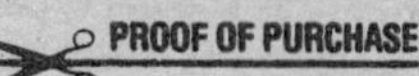

This special collection will not be sold in retail stores and is only available through this exclusive offer:

Send your name, address and zip or postal code, along with six proof-of-purchase coupons from any Silhouette Romance published in June, July and/or August, plus $2.50 for postage and handling (check or money order—please do not send cash) payable to Silhouette Reader Service to:

In the U.S.
Free Book Offer
Silhouette Books
901 Fuhrmann Blvd.
Box 9055
Buffalo, NY 14269-9055

In Canada
Free Book Offer
Silhouette Books
P.O. Box 609
Fort Erie, Ontario
L2A 5X3

(Please allow 4-6 weeks for delivery. Hurry! Quantities are limited. Offer expires September 30, 1990.)

DJC-1A